WITHDRAWN

CRY LONESOME
AND OTHER ACCOUNTS OF THE
ANTHROPOLOGIST'S PROJECT

CRY LONESOME
AND OTHER ACCOUNTS OF THE ANTHROPOLOGIST'S PROJECT

MILES RICHARDSON

STATE UNIVERSITY OF NEW YORK PRESS

Illustrations by Mary Lee Eggart

"I'm So Lonesome I Could Cry," by Hank Williams, ©1949, renewed 1976, and "Men With Broken Hearts," by Hank Williams, ©1951, renewed 1979, are reprinted with the permission of Acuff-Rose Music, Inc.-Hiriam Music, Inc.

Published by
State University of New York Press, Albany

For information, address State University of New York
Press, State University Plaza, Albany, N.Y., 12246

Library of Congress Cataloging-in-Publication Data

Richardson, Miles, 1932–
    Cry lonesome and other accounts of the anthropologist's project /
Miles Richardson; illustrations by Mary Lee Eggart.
        p.   cm.
    Includes bibliographical references.
    ISBN 0-7914-0405-6. — ISBN 0-7914-0406-4 (pbk.)
    1. Anthropologists — Fiction.   I. Title.
    PS3568.I3188C79   1990
813'.54—dc20

10   9   8   7   6   5   4   3   2   1

To you and me
in our silent anonymity
and to the I
who struggles within.

CONTENTS

ACKNOWLEDGMENTS

Many people have contributed to these accounts in many ways, and I rejoice in their wonderful grace. Gilbert Kushner, Dan Ingersoll, Gregory Reck, and Barbara Tedlock read the entire manuscript and offered helpful suggestions on organization and style. My colleagues in our unique juxtaposition of geography and anthropology have assisted in ways they may not recognize—but always helpful; Don Vermeer (now at George Washington University) and Jill Brody have more than once come to the rescue with an appropriate observation or a gracious commentary. George Thomas and Albon Quarles, friends from childhood, have kept the faith alive throughout the years. My literary groups has permitted me to practice different versions on them during our Saturday readings, and Ed Rozicka read the novella with a thoughtful eye. Beverly Jarrett lent support to this project in an earlier stage; Esther Wilcox expertly read the final manuscript. Rosalie Robertson of the State University of New York Press has taken the lead in getting the project from manuscript to published book, and for that I will be forever grateful. Finally, Valerie, my wife, and Victoria, Penn, and Stanley, my children, are so much a part of me that at times the lines dividing us disappear and anything that I do rebounds on them. May this rebound be to their credit.

INTRODUCTION

Since Adolf F. Bandelier wrote *The Delight Makers* in 1890, ethnographers have turned to fiction to make their writing about the people they study come alive. They have discovered that no matter how carefully they collect the facts of a people's existence, the sweat of a hunt on the African plain, the joy of a birth in an Amazonian hut, or the ecstasy of possession within a Haitian village, the sweat, the joy, the ecstasy disappear in the inscription of those facts on the cold pages of an ethnographic report. People whom they have come to know so well in the course of their study become, in the prose of ethnography, nameless others, separated by the passive voice of conventional science from both the ethnographer and the intended reader.

With fiction, ethnographers have found a writing that bridges the distance between the reading self and native other. By shifting the narrative point of view from that of the ethnographic observer who resides off the page in omniscient splendor to that of a participant who copes within the text in a condition of uncertainty, by allowing that participant to speak and be spoken to, but most of all, by bestowing upon the participant a name—/Qui, the Bushman; Daeyama, the Yąnomamö; Toussaint, the Haitian—the ethnographer creates an immediacy that gives life to an entombed prose (Richardson 1989).

Since Bandelier's day, ethnographers as fiction writers have achieved considerable success. Oliver La Farge's novel of Navaho life, *Laughing Boy* (1929), won a Pulitzer Prize, and more recently Hilda Kuper's *Bite of Hunger* (1965), and particularly her play, *A Witch in my Heart* (1970), have gained recognition for their portrayals of African society. A measure of their achievement is the emergence of a new genre of writing, called broadly, "narrative anthropology" (Reck 1983), or more narrowly, "ethnographic fiction" (Langness and Frank 1978; Schmidt 1981). Despite a not unexpected by-product of this success—a debate on "what is ethnographic fiction?" (Schmidt 1984)—the focus of the fiction is on the people the ethnographer writes about, the "natives." Curiously, with the exception of

Oliver La Farge's *Door in the Wall* (1965), Laura Bohannan's *Return to Laughter* (1954), and Barbara Pym's asides about the goings-on at the Institute of African Studies, the author of the ethnography, the who of the self who does the writing, has remained largely outside of fictional treatment. Even when the ethnographer returns to write sensitive stories about his own, "other" culture (Stewart 1989), it has been left to the expository essay of reflexive anthropology to reflect upon the ethnographer at work, writing (Clifford and Marcus 1986; Geertz 1988).

Notwithstanding the contributions of this most recent moment in anthropological discourse, an unfortunate side effect of its learned text has been the objectification of ethnographer. The refractive glare of reflecting upon reflections threatens to dissipate the sweat, the joy, the ecstasy of the anthropological endeavor. Having brought life to the native, we now transfigure the ethnographer into an object, and a self-serving one at that! The image of the ethnographer as an object resides at some distance from that of the ethnographer engaged in recording the pursuit of a giraffe across the Kalahari, the pride in a new father's eyes along the banks of the Orinoco, and the arrival of the sacred *loa* under a brush shelter near Mirebalais. In the same spirit that ethnographers have turned to fiction to present a participant view of the people they observe, so I turn to it to offer an account of the anthropologist.

The accounts of the anthropological self offered here, as with the alien self itself, exhibit several peculiarities. The accounting is rendered in first person essay and in third person fiction; story lines are extended into citations, footnotes, and appendices; and the narrator of two of the stories has the same name as the author of the essay, which is the same name as Case #3, the retardate in "Gug Jjjur." The mutilated voices of Case #3 and of the girl called, they say, "Rosie," are the fragmentary discourse of postmodernity; but the narrator-author is a child of the preindustrial South, whose father spoke in tongues or not at all; and even as the words talk, Miguel de Unamuno, the Basque professor of Greek at the University of Salamanca, agonizes at the grave of Hank Williams, the hillbilly existentialist from Mt. Olive, Alabama, who choked to death on his own vomit.

Why this intentional mixing of the scholarly and the fictive? This collapsing of biography and myth? This juxtaposition of the *castellaño* and the redneck? This "blurring of the genres?"—to use Clifford Geertz's apt phrasing (1983:19–37).

The intent is to raise doubts about the bridge that purports to span the distance between us, between you and me, between the writer and reader. To raise this doubt, boundaries between essay and fiction are blurred, and characters are put into situations where words turn on them or fail them, or they, in turn, give up on words and turn to silence to gain contact with others. In contrast to ethnographic fiction, which seeks to transform the exotic other of distant cultures into "realistic" humans, the attempt here is an ethnography of the anthropologist, of a self who writes of others, whose claim to selfhood resides in what that self writes, that is, speaks. And the anthropologist is the native, situated at home, not in the field, but at work at home, in his university, among the people from whom he has sprung, the very people whose culture is so at odds with the mission of his discipline.

Why this concern about words? For two reasons, one as old as anthropology, or at least Boasian anthropology, and the other as recent as postmodernity.

A central theme in the work of Franz Boas and his students was to document the diversity of cultures and to demonstrate that cultures form meaningful patterns. In that documentation, however, they came to argue that the meaning in the patterning is arbitrary. By this, they meant cultures vary in their meanings neither because of racial causes nor because of environmental determinants, but because of historically derived imperatives. What one culture conceives as fundamental, another ignores as trivial, what one boasts as achievement, another shames as infantile, and what one erects as factual, another dismisses as fairy tales. Cultures, coercive though they may be, are, nonetheless, as truthful as they claim to be. Cultures, a Boasian in the fullness of the paradigm might have said, are rhetorical devices. And today, Richard Rorty, the philosopher, informs us that the goal of knowledge is not to discover external truth but to continue a conversation (1979). And this heralds in postmodernity (Huyssen 1986).

The postmodern world, the world of you and me in the today that collapses around us, is a plurality of fragments that generates "a radical instability of meaning" (Cosgrove 1989). The postmodern world is more voice than substance; consequently, its anthropology "is the study of man 'talking'"[1] (Tyler 1986:23). To be is to speak.

The postmodern statement that the proper study of mankind is talk is but the most recent restatement of the human project, a project that began in the Pleistocene Eden, when we first strode across the African savanna, babies at our breasts, loved ones at our sides, and words—however garbled and hesitant—beguiling us even then with their transcendent ethereality. With outrageous promises that we might live forever, words lured us from the warmth of the primate troop to encase each of us in loneliness. To be, we must speak, but to speak is to risk alienation.

"Humanity is foremost conscious of itself as a community of language," writes Ernst Behler (1987:205) in summarizing the current debate between deconstruction and hermeneutics, between the Frenchman Jacques Derrida and the German Hans-Georg Gadamer, between, to put words to it, *écriture* and *Schrift*. Yet, language "is not a system of identities, but one of differences" (1987:202); words are what other words are not. May we not wonder, then, if language is, indeed, a bridge that we, you and I, build over the chasm of otherness? Or is it a barrier that cuts us off from the possibility of ever expressing that which we long to tell one another? Yet we, you and I, protest. The *speaker* speaks. The bipedal primate that crossed the savanna on its way to the moon reaches forth with the mammalian hand; *el hombre de carne y hueso*, Unamuno joins us in affirmation, the man of flesh and bone, lives.

The fiction in *Cry Lonesome* is factual. The excavation techniques described in "The Museum" and employed in "Cry Lonesome"; the details of the Chimp-O-Mat in "Gug Jjjur"; the painting by Ladislas de Czachorski on the wall in "Los Desconocidos"; and, in "Cry Lonesome," the forensic procedures followed to profile the body at the Howard place, the grammar of the creole French spoken by a self-proclaimed Parisian, and the burning of the woods in Fredonia Parish by those who live there in animosity and joy are all products of research no less committed to accuracy than those in conventional ethnography. Items in the biographies of the anthropologists in the stories come inspired from the men who first brought anthropology to the South—men, competent, well trained, and real, such as Frank Essene of the University of Kentucky, Charles Fairbanks of the University of Florida, Tom Campbell of the University of Texas, and William Haag of Louisiana State University—men who excavated an archaeological site one day, taught a linguistics class the next, and built programs up from nothing in an environment hostile to the anthropological mission. Other figures who appear, Rosie in "Don't Cry," Francine Boasz-Sauvage in "Gug Jjjur," and Seneca in "The Myth-Teller," are in varying degrees composites of acquaintances, real and fanciful. Only Joanna in "Cry Lonesome" is purely fiction, only she and the characters called "Miles."

Blurring the genres—mixing footnotes with dialogue, exposition with characterization, and paradox with corn pone—renders problematic our claims to reality. In so doing, it requires that we, together in our separate loneliness, continually speak, even in silence. In speaking, we narrate, and in our narration, in the characters we author, we endeavor to be. Ethnographically grounded in the American South and in Spanish America, two cultures in their own way as exotic as that of any New Guinea cannibal with a bone through his nose, the characters in these accounts fumble in a language, imperfect and irredeemable, to ask how is it that we, you and I, self and other, are?

NOTE

1. "That is, speaking and writing" (Tyler 1986, 46, note 1).

REFERENCES

Bandelier, Adolf F. 1890. *The Delight Makers*. New York: Dodd, Mead and Co.

Behler, Ernst. 1987. "Deconstruction versus hermeneutics: Derrida and Gadamer on text and interpretation." *Southern Humanities Review* XXI(3):201–223.

Bohannan, Laura (Elenore Smith Bowen). 1954. *Return to Laughter.* New York: Harper & Row.

Clifford, James and George E. Marcus, eds. 1986. *Writing Culture: The Poetics and Politics of Ethnography.* Berkeley: University of California Press.

Cosgrove, Dennis. 1989. Public Address. Department of Geography and Anthropology, Louisiana State University, Baton Rouge, LA

Geertz, Clifford. 1983. "Blurred genres: The refiguration of social thought." *Local Knowledge*, pp. 19–35. New York: Basic Books.

——. 1988. *Works and Lives: The Anthropologist as Author.* Stanford: Stanford University Press.

Huyssen, Andreas, 1986. *After the Great Divide: Modernism, Mass Culture, Postmodernism.* Bloomington: Indiana University Press.

Kuper, Hilda, 1965. *Bite of Hunger.* New York: Harcourt, Brace, and World.

——. 1970. *A Witch in My Heart.* Oxford University Press.

La Farge, Oliver. 1929. *Laughing Boy.* Boston: Houghton Mifflin.

——. 1965. *Door in the Wall.* Boston: Houghton Mifflin.

Langness, L. L. and Geyla Frank. 1978. "Fact, fiction, and the ethnographic novel." *Anthropology and Humanism Quarterly* 3(1&2):18–22.

Reck, Gregory. 1983. "Narrative anthropology." *Anthropology and Humanism Quarterly* 8(1):8–12.

Richardson, Miles. 1989. "Point of view in anthropological discourse." In Philip A. Dennis and Wendell Aycock (eds.) *Literature and Anthropology*, pp. 31–40. Lubbock, Texas: Texas Tech University Press.

Rorty, Richard. 1979. *Philosophy and the Mirror of Nature*. Princeton: Princeton University Press.

Schmidt, Nancy J. 1981. "The nature of ethnographic fiction: A further inquiry." *Anthropology and Humanism Quarterly* 6(1):8–18.

_____ . 1984. "Ethnographic fiction: Anthropology's hidden literary style." *Anthropology and Humanism Quarterly* 9(4): 11–14.

Stewart, John O. 1989. *Drinkers, Drummers, and Decent Folk, Ethnographic Narrative of Village Trinidad*. Albany: State University of New York Press.

Tyler, Stephen. 1986. "Post-modern anthropology." In Phyllis Pease Chock and June R. Wyman, (eds.) *Discourse and the Social Life of Meaning*, pp. 23–50. Washington, DC: Smithsonian Institution Press.

❦

THE MYTH-TELLER

"To say that every person has a fundamental project means that every individual's sense of reality rests on a particular myth"
(Charmé 1984:154).

To say that a profession has a fundamental project means that every profession rests on a particular myth. The myth that anthropology rests upon is the human myth. "The Myth-Teller" is an account of how I came to be part of anthropology's project. And it happened in the 1960s.

I was lying in the sack, staring at the walls, trying to fight the boredom of my last year in the United States Air Force. It's a hard job, fighting boredom, especially the military kind. I had tried just about everything: the bars, the hobby shop, the NCO club, the base library, even the TV in the dayroom. And the job got harder as the time to my discharge became shorter. So I was there, waiting, with a mind as empty as I could get it. Then the thought was there. Fresh. Immediate. Complete. It was almost frightening, almost unbelievable, but it became bigger, more exhilarating, more definite. Then it was me, and I decided. I was going to be an anthropologist.

My decision to be an anthropologist continues to amaze me. Even now, I'm still not sure where that idea came from. Certainly my background was not an intellectual one. My father had found his fourth grade education sufficient to move him from a tenant farm to the railroad shops. He read the newspaper and the Bible, and that's all. I had his scorn for intellectual things. I did read a lot, more than my friends, and the closest I came to an academic award was being second-to-the-topmost user of the library at David Crockett High School in Palestine, Texas. Of course, I wasn't reading Shakespeare. I like historical and frontier novels. My favorites were westerns—ones by Max Brand, Peter Field, Luke Short, Zane Grey, and especially Will James. Among my classes in school, I liked vocational argiculture. I sent off for extension pamphlets and taught myself how to recognize crazy chick disease and how to grow lespedeza. Otherwise I was content to copy term papers, make up book reports, and pester my English teacher—a sweet lady who talked about *Gone With the Wind* with tears in her eyes. So perhaps it is not surprising that in my senior year, having finished my football eligibility and with nothing else to live for, I quit high school and joined the Air Force.

Yet I know that in this background were the reasons why I became an anthropologist. The principal reason was that I was raised a Southern Baptist. You would think that a person with an intense religious upbringing would become someone compatible with that background, like a school teacher maybe, or a minister, or best of all, a football player. And people often do. One of my brothers was a preacher, and my sister married one. But it didn't work out that way for me. Actually, that's not too uncommon either. I suspect that for every minister the Southern Baptists have produced, they have turned out five atheists. Pound for pound, the Baptists have probably put more souls in hell than any other religion. And I'm one of them.

It was in my early adolescence that I discovered I was evil. Because I was evil, I was going to die. Those people who had placed their trust in their personal Savior, those who believed in him and were saved, would live forever. Not me, I was going to die. I tried hard not to be evil. I did not swear, I did not smoke, and certainly I did not drink. I didn't play dominoes nor go to the movies on Sunday. I went to church twice on Sunday plus attending the morning Sunday school and the evening Training Union. I tried to think pure thoughts. That was what really counted: what you were inside. In the Baptist doctrine good works don't save you; it is your inner surrender to Jesus, placing yourself totally in his hands, that brings you peace and everlasting life. No matter how often you go to church, how frequently you pray, or how much money you put in the collection plate, you are not saved until you turn yourself over to Jesus. The only way you know you are saved is that you *know*. But how could I be sure of such a thing? Surely a saved person always thought clean thoughts, and here I was looking at girls with lust on my mind and even stealing glances at the big-bosomed preacher's wife. How could I be saved? What could I do to escape death?

"Look to Jesus," the preacher said. But Jesus was a Lévi-Strauss paradox. Jesus-Christ-God was perfect femininity. He was kind, sweet, and full of love. Safe on his gentle breast I would lie. He so loved me that he bled and died on Calvary's tree; he was the gentle Savior who would hear my humble cry. Jesus-Christ-God was perfect masculinity. He was Father, King, Lord, and Master. He was

Victor over death and his blood was full of power. He taught gentleness and peace; he sent people to burn forever in hell. How could I touch such a figure? How could I get him to respond? I tried. I searched for a way that I could feel this God and know that I was not abandoned, and alone, and apart, and dead. I have neither tried anything harder nor wanted anything more. But I did not succeed. Then I knew I hated God.

My discovery was my salvation. Moved by the bright joy of perfect hate, I put aside Will James and began to read to find out why people were what they were, and why I was what I was. I read erratically, bits and pieces of this and that, stumbling, giving up, and then going in different directions, burning with conflicting emotions, and most of all, alone. Early in my search, I read Thomas Paine's *Age of Reason*; his challenge to established religion thrilled me. Somewhere along the line I tried E. B. Tylor's *Primitive Culture* but its nineteenth century sentence structure was too much. Later I found a list of definitions that I had carefully taken from it: "Animism: the belief in spirits; Fetishism: the worship of stones and objects." Just before I decided to become an anthropologist, I was reading travel adventure books by Dana and Ginger Lamb, husband and wife, who struggled through deserts, bandits, and inhospitable jungles to find lost cities in Latin America. The picture of myself paddling up a tropical river with some pretty blonde thing on the bow of my dugout was irresistible.

If my idea of anthropology was limited to flashes of myself in romantic situations, my feelings about it, and what I wanted from it were full and strong. I wanted freedom. To me, anthropology was liberation. It was going to free me from the view of man groveling before a God that, on the one hand was sweetly sissy and on the other remotely brutal, from a religion that makes the gentle touching between a man and a woman evil, and from a culture that wants to destroy all who read and question. It was going to free me from the memory of seeing families scratching out a living on a half-acre of scrub cotton and of hearing my father say to a neighbor, "You know Will, the principal over at Swanson's Springs? He's one of them. He comes to the front door. He doesn't go around to the back, like a good nigger."

Although anthropology was my way out, my freedom would not come from forgetting these things, nor would it come from being a part of movements to change them. I would never be a joiner. After the First Baptist Church, I had had it with formal organizations. Later, in the early 1960s when I was in graduate school, my close friend asked if I would join CORE and the sit-ins that were begin-

ning in New Orleans, but I told him no, that I was going to finish my dissertation. My freedom from the things that nearly destroyed me (and that continue to haunt me) would come from studying them, from wrestling with them in order to expose their secret. At that point, just short of stomping on them and destroying them, for some reason my private battle stopped. Today, I have no love for the Southern Baptists, but I can say Billy Graham without sneering.

After being discharged from the USAF, I took my Korean GI Bill and started out to get an education. I knew Harvard didn't want no high school dropout from Palestine, Texas, so I enrolled in a local junior college. I worked my way up from there, through undergraduate college and into graduate school. I went into the field, not with a blonde thing, but with a beautiful, brown-haired wife from England. Together we made it through. I struggled with a dissertation, and there I was, some ten years after it had happened, an anthropologist.

Now that I was one, now that I am one, what is it, being an anthropologist?

Being an anthropologist in the 1960s is to be critical: critical of one's self, of one's profession, and of one's society. Critical and suspicious, almost paranoic. The anthropologist is an academician. We are nearly always located in a university, and the nature of university life—isolated to a degree from the rest of society but dependent in large measure for its existence on that society, each year coming to grips with a new set of students, naive and sophisticated, demanding and apathetic—produces individuals drawn tight with contradictions: persons who arrogantly attack ignorance, but wistfully plead with the state legislature or the board of trustees; who teach the love of learning but jealously erect walls between academic departments; and who believe that the search for knowledge is an end in itself, but worry at night that colleagues are advancing faster, gaining more prestige, and earning more money. But the critical sensitivity of the anthropologist seems to go beyond that of the academician. You have only to attend the annual meetings of the American Anthropological Association to realize that in the anthropologist you have more than just your ordinary, run-of-the-classroom professor.[1]

Each year, at the time of Thanksgiving, anthropologists in the United States gather together in order to reexamine their collective soul. In search of expiation, individuals stand before their colleagues and accuse each other of exploiting the people whom they study for their own selfish advancement, of being unwitting tools of neocolonial powers, and worse, of being committed counter-subversives employed by the CIA or the Defense Department to study ways in which the United States can continue to maintain control over its client countries. Strong stuff for a boy from East Texas. To be sure, such self-vilification is not restricted to anthropologists; other professional societies also annually lay out their reason for being and pick it apart, looking for defects. And there are anthropologists, perhaps the confident minority, who feel no need for self-analysis and attend the meetings in order to exchange ideas with their friends. Yet the accusations that anthropologists hurl at each other contrast so sharply with the image of the anthropologist as a sympathetic spokesman for the small, the weak, and the forgotten that I must try to explain it.

That's a big order. Such an explanation must examine the makeup of academia and of American society. Like everyone else, anthropologists are part and parcel of the society in which they live (Wolf 1969). No more than their informants can anthropologists escape the biases of their home culture. Also, anthropologists vary; therefore, their discontent varies. Do the physical anthropologist (the solid scientist), the archeologist (the dirt scientist), and the linguist (the elegant scientist) share the same discontent of the ethnologist (the uncertain scientist)? Perhaps in a way they do; they are all concerned about the future of anthropology. Yet probably because I am one, I cannot escape the feeling that we ethnologists are at least more vocal about what worries us. Indeed, we occupy a key position within the science. Because we outnumber anthropologists in the other specialities and because we have the general knowledge necessary to teach the introductory course, ethnologists are frequently the persons through whom the student meets anthropology. The student can specialize in one of the other fields, but the student will enter that field with an ethnological notion of what anthropology is about. So, although my partial explanation of anthropological self-criticism will limit itself to the ethnologist, it should be applicable to the rest of anthropology.

The distinguishing feature of ethnological research is ethnographic fieldwork. In the field, the relationship most critical to the ethnographer, the one that changed him from tourist to ethnographer, is the relationship with an informant. Whenever you think of the ethnologist in the field, you think of an ethnographer talking long hours with an informant. Ethnographers do many other things. We collect figures about rainfall, crop yield, population density, migration, educational levels, and per capita income; we scan newspaper articles about local issues, important persons, and recent events; and we read historical accounts about past patterns of kinship, religious life, social stratification, and livelihoods. We watch to see how busy the market is, how friends behave, what happens at the soccer match, if men drink on Sunday, and whether the devout are always women. But sooner or later, being ethnographers, we feel that we must spend more time with informants, for the informant possesses the type of knowledge that we must have to understand this community.

Who is this person who defines, even creates, the ethnographer?[2] First, he or she is an informant, not an informer. An informer squeals to the cops. He passes on information about the activities of criminals to the police, and then the police arrest the criminals. An informant may pass on information about illegal activity to the ethnographer, but the ethnographer never arrests anyone. The informant is not an informer partly because the ethnographer is not a cop. This means that the ethnographer defines the informant. How can that be? If the informant defines the ethnographer, and the ethnographer defines the informant, how do they ever find each other? Sometimes they don't. Only after considerable trial and error does the ethnographer-informant relationship emerge.

The informant is not a subject. A subject is a person, or an animal, perhaps even a plant, that the experimenter removes from its natural surroundings and puts into a laboratory so that the experimenter is better able to control the variables that may influence the subject's response. To avoid subject bias, the experimenter sometimes tells the subject—when it is a person—that the experimenter is testing one response when in reality he is testing another. An informant is always a person, never an animal, who cannot exist apart from natural surroundings. We ethnographers may deceive the informant, but we do so at our peril, for the informant is free to reciprocate and deceive us.

The informant is not an interviewee. An interviewee answers questions, frequently highly structured, that an investigator asks, or frequently reads, from a form. This exchange, the interview, may last for as long as two or three hours, but often it is shorter; when it is finished, so is the tie between the interviewee and the investigator. Only the single strand of the interview connects them, but several stands tie the ethnographer and the informant together. An informant talks with the ethnographer about a wide range of topics, wandering here, backtracking there. The ethnographer listens more than he talks. When the conversation gradually ends, the ethnographer may ask the informant, Who in the local community is a good doctor? What is the best day to go the the market? And could he keep an eye on the ethnographer's house while the ethnographer goes to the capital for the next two days? The informant may ask, Does the United States still have the death penalty? Why are so many black people poor in America? And could the ethnographer give him a ride to the city?

The informant is not necessarily a friend. The ties that bind the ethnographer and the informant may create a friendship: it is difficult to see how an ethnographer or an informant could work with someone he hates. Yet, the relationship in itself is not one of friendship. The ethnographer must ask probing questions. We cannot, as one does with friends, accept the informant as the person he is, but the ethnographer must find out—we have to find out—why the informant believes what he does. We go to the informant seeking knowledge, and the informant becomes our instructor.

The informant is the teacher of the ethnographer. His job is to teach this stranger all that he knows. He explains the strategy of building a house, the characteristics of an extended family, and the meaning of the festival of the dead; he details how he makes pottery, how he reckons kin, and how he confronts sorrow; and he ponders with the ethnographer why cattle are sacred, why brothers are loyal, and why flowers are evil. For his job as teacher, the informant may be paid, not only in favors but also in cash. But he is not an employee; the ethnographer cannot fire him. With the informant as his teacher, the ethnographer struggles to comprehend the details and the meanings of a culture in which we are students. In the concrete facts of this particular culture, in the knowledge of this particular informant, there is somewhere, if only we were wise enough to see it, a key to the whole human story (Geertz 1965).

Without informants, we ethnographers cannot carry out our task. Ethnographers can go only so far with figures, newspapers, histories, and even with observations. To complete our work, we must turn to the informant; without the informant, we cannot be ethnographers.

Because the informant is so central to the ethnographer's reason for being, any change in the informant or in his relationship to the ethnographer, and any change in his society's relationship to the ethnographer's, will create anxiety in the ethnographer, and through the ethnographer, stress in ethnology, and ultimately conflict in anthropology. This is what has happened, and this is why anthropology's self-criticism is at its present strident pitch.

The traditional pattern of relationships between the informant and the ethnographer, like so many of our activities, grew out of the nineteenth century. This was a vigorous period of development for Western civilization. Externally, it was characterized by renewed expansion, by a rejuvenated colonialism; internally it was marked by the development of academic disciplines, one of which was anthropology. As anthropology developed into a science, it became more and more conscious of the need to collect hard data against which it could check its various theories about the biological and cultural development of humanity. Because Western civilization was only one array of data among many, only one culture in a world of cultures, anthropologists needed data outside of Western civilization. Earlier, they had relied on the accounts of travelers and missionaries; now they began to collect the data themselves. Because of the state of the world (the ordered relationships among societies, the facilities that the growing number of anthropologists had access to, and the development of transportation), the ethnographers were now able to go to other societies and to study their ways of life. Many of these societies were subordinate to one or another of those that comprised Western civilization, and so at its very beginnings ethnography was the study of subjugated people controlled by the ethnographer's society. It was in this environment that the pattern of ethnographic fieldwork developed.

The setting in which the ethnographer and the informant came together was polarized by differences in power and in culture. The two societies, the ethnographer's and the informant's, were asymmetrically paired: the ethnographer's was powerful, the informant's weak. The two cultures were likewise different: the ethnographer's literate, massive, and complex; the informant's often preliterate, delicate, and direct. The two individuals were equally dissimilar: the ethnographer was white, spoke an Indo-European language, and was highly educated; the informant was black, red, or yellow, spoke Ibo, Sioux, or Yapese, and was illiterate. However, the ethnographer-informant relationship was structured opposite to the thrust of their setting. The informant occupied the higher, dominant position and the ethnographer the lower, subordinate one. As a member of a distinct, exotic culture, the informant was a man of wisdom, schooled in the traditions of his people. The ethnographer was a trained student; his education had keyed him to discover, to find out, to learn the things that the informant knew (Mead 1972).

The ethnographer was in the field to gather data to test different theories about the biological and cultural development of humans. Although these theories were most fully expressed in Western civilization, the theories—evolutionary, diffusionist, historical—were not models for Western neocolonialism. On the contrary. Seen in the context of their times, the earlier theorists were caught up in the effort to document the march of mankind, and with their theories they did battle against religious dogmatism, degeneration, and racism. Who can match their record? You have only to read the last sentence to Tylor's *Primitive Culture* to learn that anthropology is a "reformer's science," that the study of culture is a way to combat absolutism and is a path to freedom. The ideology in late nineteenth- and early twentieth-century anthropology was not the ideology of colonial oppression, but of scientific humanism (Stocking 1963, 1966).

As a result of the interplay between the ethnographer as a scientific humanist and the informant as a man of wisdom, and through their struggle to communicate across the structural gap that separated their societies, the pattern of fieldwork developed.

As early years of the twentieth century came and went, as the colonial powers fought each other for dominance over the informants' societies, we ethnographers tried to find a niche for ourselves. Guided internally by the need for scientific objectivity, we self-consciously defined ourselves as different from other whites—from the trader, the missionary, the bureaucrat—and as persons dedicated not to exploiting, not to converting, not to administering, but to understanding the informant's culture. Although in some cases heavily modified by the impact of Western civilization, the informant's culture was still complete, still with its own tools, houses, kinsmen, and religious festivals. The myths that glorified the history of his people were still fresh on his tongue; the deeds of the great heroes, men and women who fought for their culture, still sparkled in his eyes. We ethnographers took on the task of studying this culture, of describing it in all of its richness before it began to crumble and die. This task led us into the interior of the culture, and we began to see it as an elegant balance of technology, kinship, and religion, as a work of art whose beauty lay in the way in which the parts were counterbalanced and interrelated. Yet, the ethnographer's own society, powerful, aggressive, commercial (but also humane), was ripping apart this century's old protrait of harmony. Caught between a humanistic appreciation of the informant's culture and membership in a society destroying that culture, between life and death, the ethnographer searched for understanding, and perhaps forgiveness.

The ethnographer sought understanding in the theories of cultural holism and in the methodology of cultural relativism. The holistic theories viewed particular cultures as forming patterns or configurations in which cultural traits were interrelated in either a value-thematic sense or in a functional-causal one. These theories emerged as a reaction against the "shreds and patches" views of culture in which cultural traits, such as the tipi, the travois, and the circular shield were independent units that diffused across the landscape (and sometimes across oceans). Ethnologists of the earlier schools had been using cultural traits to reconstruct the history of cultures. With the exception of the Olympian figure of Alfred L. Kroeber, ethnologists of the holistic school had little interest in the native past and were downright hostile to the idea of cultural evolution. They also seemed uninterested in the ways in which the informant's culture responded to its position at the bottom of the asymmetrical power structure. When they did write about change, it was into the specific past of particular cultures that they looked, as in the case of Africanisms; or it was how individuals in the subordinate society were becoming members of the superordinate society, as in the case of acculturation. This was true of the value-thematic-configurationist school in the United States; the British function-alist approach had even less use for history. "Pseudo-history" was what A. R. Radcliffe-Brown called the "efforts of the cultural histo-rians" (1952:3). Working at a time when their own society was penetrating into the societies of their informants, the holistic ethnologists paradoxically adopted a timeless view of culture. A par-ticular culture was a beautiful monad, a configuration of balanced interrelationships, vibrant, delicate, but contained.

Given such a view of culture, the methodological premise of cultural relativism was a logical development. As a tool for re-search, cultural relativism said that to understand any one particu-lar aspect of a culture, you had to see how it was related to the other aspects. To understand the Plains Indians' response to death—the gashing of heads and legs, the cutting off of fingers, the destruction of the dead person's lodge, the reluctance of the widow to leave the grave—you had to see how these traits were related to the overall pattern of Dionysian individualism in Plains Indian culture. And to understand the Pueblo Indians' reaction to death—a somber fun-eral feast, the ceremonial closing of the lodge door, prohibiting the dead from reentering his home, the firm speech of the chief telling the bereaved that the dead is gone, and "They shall not remember any more,"—you must view these traits against the Apollonian har-mony of Pueblo culture (Benedict 1934:110–112).

As a tool for research, cultural relativism was a significant ad-vance in ethnography. And it remains so today. It belongs to that set of ethnographic core values that advocates taking cultures as they come, do not prejudge them, and do not impose your own ethnocentric categories upon them. To comprehend any item of a people's culture, you have to view that item in its sociocultural con-text. Cultural relativism is as much a part of the ethnographer's tool kit as are field notes, tape recorders, and cameras.

But cultural relativism was more than a methodological tool for research; it was a moral justification for being anthropologists. Caught in the interplay between scientific humanism, the drive for human freedom, and the encounter with the living, exotic culture threatened by the same civilization that produced the drive, ethnog-raphers found a sense of mission in cultural relativism. Their mis-sion was to preach the doctrine of cultural differences, to lecture to their own society that there is no one path to the solution of human problems. They spoke clearly, "Here is a way of life that through the centuries has found some of the secrets of human existence. The way of our society is not the only way. Look upon this culture and be humble." This was the ethnographer's reason for being: a sort of cultural interpreter who sought to bring the intricate beauty of a fully integrated culture to the notice of his people, so that those who governed would be less arrogant and would administer their power with more sympathy.

The cultural relativists did not study how the power of their own society structured the cultures of their informants; rather, they attacked the problem of power obliquely. Horrified by the ethnocentricism of their own colonialist society, the cultural relativists protested that all cultures express equally valid solutions to the human problem and that people (and especially ethnographers) cannot be God and decide which culture is the best. Since the cultures that they studied were still whole, distinct cultures (or could be so reconstructed from the accounts of older informants), they felt strong in their arguments. Perhaps they were naive. But they were the first people in history to immerse themselves systematically, consciously, into a totally foreign culture for the explicit purpose of understanding that culture on its own terms, without any official purpose other than being an ethnographer, without any cultural hull they could hide in when the going got rough—naked, exposed, raw. Reborn by the field experience, they returned from that experience as a new breed of humans. Their hope, their mission, lay in convincing other people of the validity of that experience.

Such were the ethnographers before World War II and before the Nazis. Out of the spread of Western neocolonialism and from the development of anthropology as a discipline, they evolved a new method of learning: fieldwork. Fieldwork began as a means of gathering data to prove or disprove theories of biological and cultural evolution. In time it developed into a fixed pattern with a theory of cultures, with a methodological tool, and with a moral justification. Practiced most brilliantly by Margaret Mead, it was described most romantically by Bronislaw Malinowski:

> Soon after I had established myself in Omarakana (Trobriand Islands), I began to take part, in a way, in the village life, to look forward to the important or festive events, to take personal interest in the gossip and the developments of the small village occurrences; to wake up every morning to a day presenting itself to me more or less as it does to the native. I would get out from under my mosquito net, to find around me the village life beginning to stir, or the people well advanced in their working day according to the hour and also to the sea-

son, for they get up and begin their labours early or late, as work presses. As I went on my morning walk through the village, I could see intimate details of family life, of toilet, cooking, taking of meals; I could see the arrangements for the day's work, people starting on their errands, or groups of men and women busy at some manufacturing tasks. Quarrels, jokes, family scenes, events usually trivial, sometimes dramatic but always significant, formed the atmosphere of my daily life, as well as of theirs. It must be remembered that as the natives saw me constantly every day, they ceased to be interested or alarmed, or made self-conscious by my presence, and I ceased to be a disturbing element in the tribal life which I was to study, altering it by my very approach, as always happens with a new-comer to every savage community. In fact, as they knew that I would thrust my nose into everything, even where a well-mannered native would not dream of intruding, they finished by regarding me as part and parcel of their life, a necessary evil or nuisance, mitigated by donations of tobacco (1961:7–8).

The traditional pattern of fieldwork—the asymmetrical pairing of the two societies, the great differences between the two cultures, the informant as a man of wisdom with the ethnographer as his student, and the accompanying moral justification—became a part of the subculture of ethnology and of anthropology. This was the image that I carried into the field, and like many of my contemporaries, I found it archaic.

I was just beginning to wake up when a great voice boomed into the patio and blasted me into my mosquito net. "People of San Pedro. Arise! Men to the fields. Children to school. And come to mass Sunday. If you don't, you will turn into Communists or Protestants." A nice guy in other ways, the new priest enjoyed hearing his voice amplified to god-like proportions by the loud speaker located on top of the church steeple, a block from my house. I fought my way through the mosquito net and got my feet on the floor. I leaned down and pulled my machete out from under the mattress. I looked at it a minute, vaguely wondering what I would do if some of the thieves that supposedly lived in San Pedro ever decided to rob me. Doña Leonor had warned me about them, "Listen *mister*, you've got to be more careful. Yesterday I passed by your house and saw that your window was open. The thieves will look in and see all your things, and at night they will climb over the patio wall and cut your throat." I hung the machete up and let my dog out into the back yard. He was a big, black, but very friendly Labrador that in a period of homesickness, I had named "Tex." He had a loud, deep bark that Doña Leonor approved of. I belched up last night's *aquardiente* and almost threw up as the sweet, sticky taste of white rum spread into my mouth. I turned on my water faucet and looked with dismay at the brown sludge that came out of it. With my teeth still furry, I went down the street to buy the morning bread. "The bread hasn't come yet, *míster*," snapped the store lady. She turned to another customer, "Look as this, would you." She spread the newspaper out before his disbelieving eyes. "Colombia! What a rotten country." she exclaimed. I peeked over their shoulders at the front page photograph of a naked body with its head by its feet. The caption explained that a bandit group, led by *Capitán Tarzán*, had murdered peasants in a mountain village and had mutilated the bodies. The store lady went on several minutes about how the rich were hiring the bandits to drive peasants away from their land, so that the rich could buy the property at a bargain price.

Later that morning, I thought I would be like Malinowski and walk through the village, etc., so I got Tex and went out. The men had left for their work, the women were cleaning house behind closed doors and windows, and the kids were in school. But at least Tex enjoyed it. Being a Labrador, he couldn't resist jumping into a large spring boxed in with concrete. As I called him out, a man walking by muttered, "Gringos! Letting their dogs dirty the water people bath in." Back at my house, I was writing field notes, when Seneca came. "I can't go with you today to visit the tobacco factory. I've got to go to Tuluá and get some medicine for my mother. We're out of money. Look, doctor, could you loan me two hundred pesos? Thanks. Look, doctor, could you speak to your *jefe*, to the chief of your organization, about me. I know that if you will do that, he'll hire me. You'll do that, will you? That's all it will take. Just a word on your part. You are out of cigarettes? Here, have one of mine."

Having graciously donated me his tobacco, Seneca left. Lighting the cigarette, I stood in the doorway and looked at the deserted plaza and across the plaza to the valley and then at the Andes mountains, rising up to meet the clouds. I shut the door, picked up my guitar, and, fumbling the chords of a

Hank Williams tune, thought long thoughts about Palestine, Texas, and home.

The traditional model of fieldwork, up in the clouds of Malinowskian romanticism, did not signify when applied to the reality of the world emerging in the 1950s and the 1960s. The traditional patterns grew out of the neocolonialism of the late nineteenth century; the new pattern of fieldwork struggles to take form in the revolutionary turbulence of the second half of the twentieth century.

The setting in which the ethnographer and the informant work today is still polarized by differences in power and in culture. These differences are far less sharp than before. The two societies remain asymmetrically paired, but the informant's society has gained considerable power while the ethnographer's society has lost some. The society of the informant is now at least nominally free of the ethnographer's and, in some cases, it may exercise considerable independence for varying lengths of time. The Arab oil embargo of 1973–74 is one example. How much real power and true freedom the developing societies have is difficult to assess. Yet in comparison with their status in the traditional pattern of fieldwork, the societies of the informants have gained power.

Moreover, the ethnographer of today comes from a background considerably different from that traditionally associated with anthropology in the United States. At least according to anthropological folklore, ethnographers of the older tradition were largely from the upper classes. Their families were families of solid substance, or they were connected to ones that were. Several had wealthy patrons. The environment in which they grew up was an intellectual one; their relatives were people who valued learning. Nearly all were born in the great cities of the northeast, and ethnically they often were Jewish, German, or Old-American. Frequently, they were close, personal friends or close, personal enemies. Beginning after World War II and especially since the Korean War, changes in American society, the rising standard of living, more governmental support for education, and increased urbanization have widened the recruiting base for anthropology (Nash and Wintrob 1972). No doubt many continue to come from the upper classes, but also many emerge from the lower levels. They come from backgrounds that ordinarily do not supply academicians. While probably few are ex-Southern Baptists, many are children of parents who earned modest incomes and who placed little faith in education. A substantial number were born in smaller cities and towns in different parts of the country, and while still predominantly white, they are more eth-

nically diverse than were previous anthropologists. Compelled by
the contradictory forces within them, they break the ties with their
background and look for a style of life to replace the one of their
rough and ready fathers. They adopt the academic style, but it
wears unevenly. They overcompensate here, undercompensate there.
They are what they scorn in others; they are status-aspiring; they
are Archie Bunkers with Ph.D.s. When they go into the field, they
carry these scars with them. Insecure in themselves, perhaps they
find insecure people to study.

The same changes that have broadened the recruiting base for
anthropologists have also popularized anthropology. Earlier, general knowledge about anthropology was restricted to a few who believed that anthropology was to the social sciences what physics was
to the natural sciences: intellectual, competent, cool. Currently,
while still retaining some of its elitist charm and derring-do, anthropology, like the submarine sandwich, is becoming massified. It
seems to be on its way to becoming just another social studies re-
quirement that freshmen must take, with the anthropologist just
another vague, gray figure, barely perceptible against the backdrop
of blackboard and chalk dust.

Similarly, the informant—the embodiment of a culture that
through the centuries has worked out its deep, smooth solutions to
the problems of human existence—is now a tarnished figure barely
visible against the backdrop of television, rock music, Charlton Heston, and beer bottles. Even though his race is often different, cultur-
ally the informant and his society resemble more and more the
ethnographer and his society. While in recent times the ethnographer's society may have secured special forms of music, new types
of literature, and new clothing styles from the informant's society,
these are small in comparison to the current massive export of cultural items, from computers to Bat Man, from the ethnographer's
society to the informant's (Camacho 1972). The ethnographer is
finding that the informant's culture contains the very attributes
that he tried to avoid by leaving his own small town: getting ahead
even if it means walking on people; forgetting kinship ties with the
poor and maximizing those with the rich; ranking men on how well
they can fight and fuck, and ranking women on how empty-headed
they can pretend to be; and damning all who study and question.

Either because of the wholesale incorporation of cultural
traits or because of the more subtle but effective process of moderni-
zation, the informant's culture becomes an impoverished version of
the ethnographer's (Richardson 1967). The sphere of the informant's
knowledge is less and less distinctive and more and more restricted.

It becomes more difficult for the pair to perform the roles of the man of wisdom instructing his most talented student. Occasionally the structure collapses, and the pair find themselves playing out the farce of the ethnographer as patron and the informant as the unfortunate, who begs favors. The proud primitive now whines; the sensitive student now commands. The massification of the ethnographer. The proletarianization of the informant. Disillusion. Bitterness.

The collapse of the traditional pattern of fieldwork against the reality of the contemporary field experience is a major cause of the feeling of disaster and guilt that permeates ethnology, and through ethnology, American anthropology. The traditional pattern justified the ethnographer's being an ethnographer through the message of cultural relativism which rested on the theory of cultures, of shining monads, intricate, complete, dazzlingly crystal against the black sky of nature. Once these monads began to merge into a uniform, brown sameness, how could the doctrine of cultural differences have any appeal? Once the informant was a man who fought with Geronimo. Now he is a Saturday drunk in the white man's jail. How can the ethnographer profess that every culture has equally valid solutions to the human problems? How can the ethnographer find a special niche for himself in the informant's society? He bumps into others seeking the same niche, sociologists, political scientists, and local ethnographers (the last, exasperated by the constant demands of foreign social scientists, wish that they all would take their problems and go elsewhere). How can the ethnographer be reborn by immersing himself in a truly different culture, when nearly all cultures are becoming the same and the informant looks more and more like the people from across the tracks? How can he handle the guilt generated by seeing how his society exploits the informant's society, when there is no flash of exotic culture to lure his attention away from shacks built from cardboard and lives built from braggadocio and abnegation?

He can't. The collapse of the traditional model of fieldwork, with its moral justification grounded on the theory and experience of cultural differences, against the uncompromising reality of the contemporary structure has left the ethnographer, ethnology, and to a degree, anthropology without a sense of mission. Without an implicit, shared sense of doing what is right, anthropology in the United States has become unhooked from itself. Different anthropologists race each other in their willingness to accept the most devastating criticism. Some happily agree with the sociologists that we should stop trying to be novelists and become scientists (people who wear white smocks and hire interviewers). Others are painfully delighted with the assertion from minority groups that only a black can understand the soul of the black (a statement which recalls that of the white supremists who say that only the Southerner can understand the South). Still others suicidally rejoice when one of their fellow anthropologists proclaims that the end of anthropology is at hand.

Currently, anthropologists are at each other's throats with three competing justifications for being an anthropologist: First, anthropology is a science and needs no other justification. It seeks to broaden and deepen human knowledge about humans through a search for general principles that are applicable to the study of any particular sociocultural system. Anthropologists as anthropologists should stay clear of political matters, such as passing resolutions about racial injustice or genocide. This is the traditional justification, and today's critics swarm around it like oilmen around sheiks. It is toy-playing in the ivory tower, or worse, its neutral stance is a front for the establishment. Second, anthropology should be an applied science. While there is nothing wrong with studying baboons, Folsom points, Adena pottery, and cross-cousin marriage, the basic purpose of anthropology is the application of its knowledge to easing the pain of transition from the primitive-peasant condition to the complex-modern one. At one time the applied approach was the radical one. Indeed, if another bit of anthropological folklore is accurate, the Society for Applied Anthropology was formed in protest to the failure of the American Anthropological Association to take the applied field seriously. Today, however, the daring young men of yesterday are the gray beards of the establishment. The best that an applied anthropologist can hope for from his critics is to be called a "liberal lackey"—a person whose heart bleeds for the underdog but whose pocketbook is filled with establishment paychecks. Third, anthropology should be in the service of the revolution. This recent justification (which like relevance and streaking is already at the what-else-is-new level) argues that not only did anthropology grow out of colonialism, but that it is also colonialistic. To regain its soul, anthropology must place itself at the service of the society it studies. It should be prepared to fight for the informant and his society—even if the informant doesn't feel like fighting. Critics quickly point to the arrogance of the revolutionary anthropologist—a person who *knows* what *his* people need. Labels like bourgeois adventurer and radical chic fly around his head and bug him constantly.

Where do we go from here? As an ethnologist, I'm not sure. Maybe that is the best way to be. I like what Dell Hymes says:

I would hope to see the consensual ethos of anthropology move from a liberal humanism, defending the powerless, to a socialist humanism, confronting the powerful and seeking to transform the structure of power. Yet one can have no illusion of unanimity on all issues. In World War I, as Norman Thomas once put it, socialists were killing each other as cheerfully as Christians. . . . In a given country three conscientious anthropolgists might choose three different loyalties—one to a government, one to a group seeking to overthrow it or to secede from its control, and one to a village that wished to be left alone by both. . . . Nor can we ignore obligations to our families, which we might put ahead of all others (Hymes 1972:52–53).

We can begin by saying goodby to Malinowskian primitive anthropology. Once we have purged ourselves of the traditional model, we are ready to accept the contemporary world on its own terms—a basic anthropological notion. When we do this, something magical happens. The real world shifts a bit, and there he is—the informant—the man of wisdom, clear and distinct, ready, if we will but listen, to instruct us once again in the old, old lesson of being human. Maybe he can't tell us everything there is to know about his culture, but he can tell us something of the mystery of the human enterprise. He is no subject or interviewee, but a person—man or woman—who knows that this is the way life is. All we need to do is to listen.

But how to listen, that's the question. As a scientist, as an applied anthropologist, as a revolutionary? What stance should the ethnographer take, not only as an ethnographer listening to an informant, but also as an anthropologist with a mission? That is a decision that each anthropologist must make in solitude. But we must expect tension among ourselves, between us and American society, and even between us and our informants and their societies—particulary their elites. As long as ethnographers continue to occupy the precarious junction between superordinate and subordinate societies, we are going to have the stomachaches of contradictions and ambiguities. These contradictions and ambiguities will make us dissatisfied, and restless, and critical, so that being an anthropologist is like being the marshall of Dodge City back in the rough and ready days of radio drama: "It's a chancy job. It makes a man watchful—and a little lonely."

There is another stance that the anthropologist might take. It is older, much older than being a pure scientist, applied scientist, or revolutionary. That is the stance of the myth-teller. The myth-teller, the epic poet, stood on the fringes of his society and told of

the great struggles between gods and humans, how they fought and
how they loved. The poet knew these experiences; he felt their heat
and pull, but something within him drove him to the margins of
society where he could see all that was happening. There he re-
corded in his head what took place. What he saw moved him. Before
him stood the great hero. Two-thirds god, the hero wanted to do everything, learn everything, and understand everything. Because of
the god-part that was in him, he could not accept death and strove
to conquer it; but because of the human-part, he failed. He was the
tragic hero, magnificent in strength, splendid in appearance,
courageous in heart, but with one fatal flaw: he was one-third man.
The myth-teller saw in the struggles of the hero the lot of man.
Man's lot is that he question; but it is equally his lot that he receive
no answer (Richardson 1972).

Being human is being heroic. Back at the time when ice
chilled the air and when great mammals trembled the earth with
their tread, the human epic began. Out of the turbulence of the
Pleistocene we arose. Firm of foot, skillful of hand, quick of thought,
and with images dazzling in our eyes, we moved out of Africa and
out of the Pleistocene, until now we have explored earth, walked on
the moon, and touched Jupiter, and beyond. We are a biological success. We have made our mark for all to see. Who can challenge what
we have done?

The reason for our success is our ability to symbolize experience, to dream of what might be and then to act as if the dreams
were real (White 1949; Burke 1966; and Duncan 1968). In us all the
flow, and crash, and thunder of the primate experience has become
externalized and objectified (Hallowell 1968; Holloway 1969; and
Richardson 1974). We have taken the private learning, the inward
emotions, the life experience of the individual primate and, through
the magic of symbols, have externalized it onto our behavior, our
sounds, and our tools. What once was mating is now marriage, what
once were calls are now words, and what once were termite sticks
are now atomic bombs.

The ability to symbolize, to have culture, has made us what
we are. We know the world because of culture; because of culture
we also know fear. The fear that we humans know is not solely the
fear of imminent danger: It is the fear of being evil, of being dead,
of being alone. While culture allows us to talk to each other, it also
prohibits us from being with one another. We can no longer reach
out and touch our other selves; we can only encounter what we imagine others to be. We can't approach our other selves directly, but
only as we symbolize the others to be: man, woman, black, white,

friend, enemy. No matter how hard we try, we cannot escape labeling and being labeled. Labeling is as much a part of us as shells are a part of turtles. Shells allow turtles to exploit a niche in the environment; culture allows us to do the same. No more than the turtle can take off his shell can humans stop symbolizing. Only when the turtle becomes extinct and we blow ourselves up will we both be free of shells and culture. Culture is our blessing; it is also our curse, our fatal flaw.

Like the hero seeking after eternal life, we seek to escape loneliness. Walled in by our prison of culture, we cannot reach others. We try, we struggle, we stick out our hands, but find nothing. But we try again, and again find nothing. What made us human, the power to envision a better world, will not let us rest. We push ourselves to the limit of our individual cells and try once more, but again there is nothing. What made us human, the ability to label and to act on those labels, guarantees that we fail.

Reality eludes us since we left the warm comfort of the primate troop. As we struggle to cope with the problem of being human, as we try to adapt to the human condition, we evolve cultural patterns that go in contradictory direction. *We are cruel.* We wage war on our own kind, shooting other people with arrows, cutting their bodies with obsidian swords, blasting them apart with land mines. We starve members of our own societies, building economic systems that produce fat billionaires and thin babies, crying in the night. We grind psyches in the grist mill of religion, tearing apart souls for the Glory of God, in the Highest. *We are magnificent.* With a digging stick and a pebble tool we beat the African savanna at its own game. With torch and red ochre we drew on the cave walls of Europe delicate pictures of wild beasts. With shining metal and finely tuned instruments we went to the moon. Before our story ends, perhaps we will feel Mars beneath us and even walk under the light of a new star. *We are love.* We are brothers; we are sisters. Listen to those of us who speak for all: "As a man I work for the party; as a poet I work for man," César Vallejo, Peruvian Marxist. "From where the sun now stands I will fight no more forever," Chief Joseph, American Indian. "Free at last! Free at last! Thank God Almighty, I'm free at last!" Martin Luther King, Jr., Southern black. We are these things and more. How can a single species do and be so many contradictory things? The ability to symbolize makes us what we are. It accounts for our successes; it is the reason for our failures. Being a human is an impossible task, but it is our task.

The anthropologist's job is to tell of that task, to glorify the species by composing and reciting with skill and passion the human myth. Like the poet recording the exploits of the epic hero, the anthropologist mythicizes the human record. He takes the discrete bits of human data, the pelvic girdle, Acheulean handaxes, Eskimo kinship, and phonemic contrast, and narrates the human story: how we came to be, how we fought in the past, how we live today. As teller of that human story, the anthropologist cannot falsify what we are. He seeks to find the full range of human variation, the cruelty, the magnificence, the love that is in us all and in all of our cultures. But the anthropologist is not a passive recorder of human data; he searches for the human secret.

As myth-teller, the anthropologist feels the heat and pull of human effort. As ethnographers, we stand between the juncture of superordinate and subordinate societies, and we experience the contradictory stresses of that position. We must not isolate ourselves from those stresses by putting on white smocks and directing interviewers from the sterile atmosphere of an air-conditioned office. If children consider us just more village idiots, if adults laugh at our childlike mistakes, if we are consistent victims of Montezuma's Revenge (or the Old World variant, the Pharoah's Curse), at least we live in the world of people. Nor can ethnographers be principally occupied with directing cultural traffic from the superordinate to the subordinate society. Neither can we forget, in our anxiety to speak for the poor, that the rich also fall within the range of human variation. To recite the human epic, the anthropologist needs the passion of the radical, the practicality of the liberal, and the detachment of the scientist. But in the end, he must remain a teller, perhaps a revolutionary teller, but a poet and not a change agent.

In telling the human myth—of how men wrestle with the problem of being human, of how people envision a society of love but live in a society of hate, of how they conceive of a collective soul but live in individual cells—the anthropologist may find his own salvation. In writing of the struggles of others, he may find ways to cope with his own demons that torture him at night. In reciting the heroism of humans, he may learn to live heroically: to know that gods live forever, but humans die bravely.

If the anthropologist does not tell the human myth, then who will?

Who will see human gentleness in a Ramapithecus jaw?
Who will look with wonder at the Sorcerer of Les Trois Frères?
Who will hunt meat with the Siriono or weep when a
    Sánchez dies?

Who will see a verb in a pebble tool, or fight for
  Papiamentu, or learn the grammar of he be gone?
Who will watch the ghosts dance?

Who will argue about the pre-Columbian chicken, or pre-
Clovis man, or maize in Africa?
Who will defend the Neanderthal?

Who will watch the bird glide over the New Guinea highlands?
Who will feast with the Yạnomamö or go north with Nanook?
Who will journey with Don Juan?

Who will record these things and more?
Who will search for the human secret? Who will tell the
  human myth?
Who will, damn it, who will?

NOTES

This account originally appeared in 1974 as "Anthropologist: The Myth Teller", *American Ethnologist*. 2:517–533. I owe a tremendous debt to Victoria Bricker, then the editor of the *American Ethnologist*, for her willingness to publish such an unorthodox article.

I completed the first draft of this article while on sabbatical leave, fall semester, 1973, and I thank Dr. Irwin A. Berg, Dean of the College of Arts and Sciences, and the administration of Louisiana State University for granting the sabbatical. Sam Hilliard, Joyce Rockwood Hudson, Valerie Richardson, and Donald Vermeer made helpful comments. I particularly thank Ward Goodenough and Charles Hudson for their encouragement and Charles for his sharp editorial eye. Illusions do not elude him. Of course, I am solely responsible for this attempt to write about anthropology.

Because being an anthropologist is an intense thing, I have tried to write intensely, and, I hope, skillfully. Maybe I'm a frustrated novelist, but I can't help but feel (along with Langness 1973) that there is a place in professional journals for articles that make the reader grunt and say goddamn. If I were still a Southern Baptist, I would say that I was writing an inspirational piece, somewhere between Billy Graham's "The Hour of Decision" and Martin Luther King's "I Have a Dream."

1. My notion of the tone of anthropology in the United States comes from attending the meetings of the American Anthropological Association and from reading the letters to the editor in the *Newsletter* and the debates that go on in *Current Anthropology*. My characterization of the background of both earlier and contemporary anthropologists draws heavily on anthropological folklore, and as folklore has purposes other than truth telling, the characterizations are no doubt inaccurate in detail. Anthropologists have pub-

lished little on their social background and their place in American society. A growing literature, however, exists on ethnographers in the field. When reading these accounts, one occasionally thinks of the reports in *True Magazine*, like "My Years Among the Man Eating Amazons of Brazil." But this literature is a far cry from, and a vast improvement over, the time not long ago when there were only Malinowski's account and the chapter on interview techniques and field relationships by Paul (1953) in *Anthropology Today*. As background material for this article, I have sampled this literature: Gerald Berreman (1962), Joseph B. Casagrande (1960), Morris Freilich (1970), I. C. Jarvie (1969), Solon T. Kimball and James B. Watson (1972), Arden R. King (1965), Peter Kloos (1969), Dennison Nash (1963), Hortense Powdermaker (1966), and George Spindler (1970).

2. The description of the informant and of the ethnographer-informant relationship draws on the literature cited above and on my fieldwork, a year and a half in Colombia (1962–1963) and three summers in Costa Rica (1967, 1972, 1973). Since 1974, I have spent a portion of nearly every summer in either Mexico or Guatemala.

REFERENCES

Aceves, Joseph B. 1974. *Identity, Survival, and Change: Exploring Social/Culture Anthropology.* Morristown, NJ: General Learning Press.

Benedict, Ruth. 1934. *Patterns of Culture.* Boston: Houghton Mifflin.

Berreman, Gerald. 1962. *Behind Many Masks.* Society for Applied Anthropology, Monograph No. 4.

Burke, Kenneth. 1966. *Language as Symbolic Action.* Berkeley: University of California Press.

Camacho, Daniel. 1972. *La dominación cultural en el subdesarrollo.* San José, Costa Rica: Editorial Costa Rica.

Casagrande, Joseph B., ed. 1960. *In the Company of Man: Twenty Portraits of Anthropological Informants.* New York: Harper Torchbooks.

Charmé, Stuart L. 1984. *Meaning and Myth in the Study of Lives.* Philadelphia: University of Pennsylvania Press.

Duncan, Hugh D. 1968. *Symbols in Society.* New York: Oxford University Press.

Freilich, Morris, ed. 1970. *Marginal Natives: Anthropologists at Work.* New York: Harper and Row.

Geertz, Clifford. 1965. "The impact of the concept of culture on the concept of man." In John R. Platt (ed.), *New Views of Man*. Chicago: University of Chicago Press.

Holloway, R. L., Jr. 1969. "Culture: A *human* domain." *Current Anthropology* 10: 395–412.

Hollowell, A. Irving. 1968. "Self, society, and culture in phylogenetic perspective." In M. F. Ashley Montagu (ed.), *Culture: Man's Adaptive Dimension*. New York: Oxford University Press.

Hymes, Dell. ed. 1972. *Reinventing Anthropology*. New York: Random House.

Jarvie, I. C. 1969. "Problems of ethnical integrity in participant observations." *Current Anthropology* 10: 505–508.

Kimball, Solon T., and James B. Watson, eds. 1972. *Crossing Cultural Boundaries: The Anthropological Experience*. New York: Chandler.

King, Arden R. 1965. "The anthropologist as man: The ultimate paradox." Paper presented at the Sixty-Fourth Annual Meeting, American Anthropologist Association, Denver, Colorado. Published version (1987) "Anthropologist as human: The ultimate paradox." *Anthropology and Humanism Quarterly 12*: 47–51.

Kloos, Peter. 1969. "Role conflicts in social fieldwork." *Current Anthropology* 10: 509–512.

Langness, L. L. 1973. "Fact, fiction, style and purpose: Some comments on anthropology and literature." Paper presented at the Seventy-Second Annual Meeting, American Anthropological Association, New Orleans, Louisiana. Published version with Gelya Frank (1978) "Fact, fiction, and the ethnographic novel." *Anthropology and Humanism Quarterly* 3:16–22.

Malinowski, Bronislaw. 1961. *Argonauts of the Western Pacific*. 1922. Reprint. New York: E. P. Dutton.

Mead, Margaret. 1972. "Fieldwork in high cultures." In Kimball and Watson (eds.), *Crossing Cultural Boundaries: The Anthropological Experience*. New York: Chandler.

Nash, Dennison. 1963. "The ethnologist as stranger: An essay in the sociology of knowledge." *Southwestern Journal of Anthropology* 19:149–167.

Nash, Dennison, and Ronald Wintrob. 1972. "The Emergence of self-conscious in ethnography." *Current Anthropology* 13: 527–542.

Paul, Benjamin. 1953. "Interview techniques and field relationships." In A. L. Kroeber (ed.), *Anthropology Today*. Chicago: University of Chicago Press.

Powdermaker, Hortense. 1966. *Stranger and Friend: The Way of an An-thropologist.* New York: W. W. Norton.

Radcliffe-Brown, A. R. 1952. *Structure and Function in Primitive Society.* London: Cohen & West.

Richardson, Miles. 1967. "The significance of the 'hole' community in anthropological studies." *American Anthropologist* 69: 41–54.

_____ . 1972. "Gilgamesh and Christ: Two contradictory models of man in search of a better world. "In Joseph B. Aceves (ed.), *Aspects of Cultural Change.* Southern Anthropological Society, Proceedings No. 6. Athens: University of Georgia Press. (Reprinted in Aceves 1974.)

_____ . 1974. "Images, objects, and the human story." In Miles Richardson (ed.) *The Human Mirror: Material and Spatial Images of Man.* Baton Rouge: Louisiana State University Press.

Spindler, George. ed. 1970. *Being an Anthropologist: Fieldwork in Eleven Cultures.* New York: Holt, Rinehart and Winston.

Stocking, George W., Jr. 1963. "Matthew Arnold, E. B. Tylor and uses of invention." *American Anthropologist* 65: 783–799.

_____ . 1966. "Franz Boas and the culture concept in historical perspective." *American Anthropologist* 68: 867–882.

White, Leslie. 1949. *The Science of Culture.* New York: Farrar, Straus and Cudahy.

Wolf, Eric. 1969. "American anthropologists and American society." In Stephen Tyler (ed.), *Concepts and Assumptions in Contemporary Anthropology.* Southern Anthropological Society, Proceedings, No. 3. Athens: University of Georgia Press.

❦

I-8[1]

Last night I couldn't decide if it were a wedding or a funeral, so I brought both roses and lilies. Now both are wilted and dry. Eaten up by the Louisiana August. Like the '60s. Say farewell to the '60s. They have been sucked dry, devoured, and are now dead.

Joanna saw it first, in 1968. It was in the *Messenger.*

Plans have been finalized for the routing of a limited access, four lane thoroughfare through Mt. Hope. Responding to concerns voiced by certain segments, Mayor Gates reassured citizens that the superhighway, numbered I-8, will be directed around residential areas. The mayor cited a corps of engineer's report that construction will affect only a small area north of Main, near the New Jersey and Atlantic plant. Likewise, it may disturb an equally small section south, along the Illinois Central tracks, known as "Reed's Town." "The coming of I-8 can only lead to the beautification of our skyline." the mayor declared.

"We will have to move," Joanna announced.

Picturing the manuscript waiting impatiently on my desk now that summer school was over, I was anxious to be off, so I didn't answer. Instead, I measured the rise of the August sun as its rays crossed the Illinois Central railroad and moved through the pecan grove at the far rear of our lot. When the sun got to the tree tops, I could go.

"We will have to move," Joanna repeated and sipped her tea, a carefully brewed Earl Gray she purchased from a specialty shop in New Orleans. "I never thought of this house as anything other than temporary. When we first came, you had your dissertation to finish, and we had to take what we could find. Now with your promotion, we want a residence more suitable to our station."

I leaned forward to squint at the sun. A couple of more yards. Getting ready, I finished my coffee. Despite years in Louisiana, I was still Texan enough to draw the line at dark roast.

"Here's a possibility," Joanna was already into the classifieds. *Three bedroom. All electric. Large lot. In Villa del Rey.* "Could that be the one I saw near the Hollingsworths'?"

"Pretty classy neighborhood."

"Why shouldn't we live near the president of the university? Instead of across the tracks from those rednecks?"

Joanna said "those rednecks" with the disdain appropriate for a self-declared liberal Unitarian from the rich side of Dallas.

"Pretty big for just the two of us," I jiggled my empty cup.

"You could have a study and," Joanna laughed with delight, "I could have a boudoir. Besides, we need a guest room."

Knowing the guest she had in mind, I asked, "Heard from your father lately?"

"As a matter of fact, I called to thank him for the tea service."

"That's nice."

"Yes, I sometimes, think—well, I hope—we might have a reconciliation. We must realize how he felt when I told him I was getting married . . ."

"To a man only five years younger than he," I finished her sentence and got up.

"Now, don't you get that hurt look."

"I won't," I replied and gave her a goodbye peck.

It was on the edge of the pecan grove by the next August—the August of 1969. It had traveled fast. When Joanna read about it the year before, it was still in Mississippi and east of the Pearl. Once over the Pearl, it raced through the pine-covered countryside of Louisiana's parishes and sped directly for the Tangipahoa. January it was at the river's edge north of town. It leaped over the river and, with great bounds, sped through the NJ&A Quarters, Main Street, Reed's Town, and the Illinois Central. Omnivorous, it fed on Lincoln High in the Quarters, and in Reed's Town, it ate the New Jerusalem Baptist, but as hungry as it was, it avoided Villa del Rey. Catching its breath for the final lunge south to New Orleans, it nibbled at the edge of the pecan grove at the back of our yard. The next day, while I watched, it vanished.

True, men in hard hats came, built frames, wove metal rods, and poured concrete. True, they worked long into the night and even through the weekends. But, their work done, they left, and from the Tangipahoa to Reed's Town, what they left in Mt. Hope was solid emptiness. Their immense creation, which stretched from house top to tree top, had no interior. Inside all that cement, rock, and sand, there was not an it, like the it that was inside a home or inside a woman.

Each morning, before I fixed breakfast, I stood on the back porch to see if it were there. Each time, there was nothing. Its absence challenged me.

"A thing of that size has got to have meaning," I said to a silent Joanna as we sat down to fruit and whole wheat toast.

She glanced at me over her tea. Then she peered into the cup
as if to divine her future. I wondered what she saw.

The house she had picked out, the all-electric, three-bedroom,
large-lot, near-University one, remained unattainable. Even with
my veteran status and with the equity in the one we lived in, I could
not secure a loan from the Mt. Hope First Federal. "We would like
to help you, Professor," Jordan Hollingsworth, brother of the silver-
haired president, assured me. "Perhaps a residence more suitable
to your income bracket." But Joanna would have no other.

I suspected that she had approached her father about a loan and
had been rebuffed. There was no more talk about reconciliation, and
I rarely saw a letter in his precision writing on her night table. Their
difficulties were deeper than our marriage. They fought over religion.
In high school she left the Methodists and became a Unitarian.
They fought over politics. A senior at Sophie Newcomb in New Orleans, she joined CORE and sent him—company executive and Republican fund raiser—news clippings of her sitting-in at lunch coun-
ters on Canal. But they had their biggest battle when she dropped
out of graduate school and left with me to do fieldwork in Mexico.
It was a full scale, nuclear-tipped exchange, and it left them both
victims. Victims of me, I more than once thought.

During the interstate's trounce through Mt. Hope, the *Messenger* had remained subdued, but, with construction safely out of
the parish, the paper regained its earlier enthusiasm. It eulogized
the governor, the congressman, the mayor, but saved its finest words
for Laird "Bubba" Woodard, of Woodard Fabrications Inc. In its testimony to the contractor's entrepreneurial skill, it even reviewed
Bubba's game-winning touchdown in the pivotal 1950 Halloween
contest against the raging Cajuns of Lafayette. It concluded by noting that, despite a full schedule, Mr. Woodard had consented to attend the official dedication cermony.

"While at first glance rituals may appear superficial, anthropologists have discovered that they often articulate a culture's
fondest hopes and its deepest fears," I recalled telling a class. So I
attended the dedication.

The ceremony had to be held more than a mile out of town
because that was the only place around Mt. Hope where the
superhighway ran at ground level. I arrived early and watched Deputy Sheriff Wright set up a barrier to divert such traffic as there
was. Behind the barrier, workmen from the city stretched a red ribbon across one lane. Shortly, led by Police Chief Andrew "Red" Gilmore astride his Harley, the official entourage arrived. Waiting for
the reporter from the *Messenger*, who was also the paper's photo-

grapher, to set up his camera, Mayor Gates passed a pair of scissors to Woodard and put his arm around Mary Ellen Hanks, who was dressed in a swimsuit with "Miss Pine Tree, 1969" draped between her ample endowments.

Camera in place, the mayor spoke with considerable enthusiasm at some length about how the interstate had already brought to Mt. Hope a sense of purpose, a definition of the future, a vision of progress and prosperity. He singled out for special praise Woodard Fabrications Inc. and even squeezed in an allusion to the founder's 1950 touchdown run. Finally, he asked that we bow our heads in prayer.

"Almighty God," the mayor began, "You who have commanded us to lay low the mountains, raise high the valley, and make straight the highway, we ask your blessings upon those who have done just that. Bless the investment bankers, the stock holders, the company executives; bless the engineering professors, the governmental officials, and the elected officers; bless the manufacturers, the distributors, and the contractors; and, Lord, we ask your special blessing upon those assembled here today to carry forth, in our humble fashion, the task you have assigned us. In Jesus's name, Amen."

In the pause that followed the prayer, Mary Ellen arched her endowments, the camera flashed, and Bubba leaned into the ribbon like it was fourth and goal on the Cajun's one. And that was that. Congratulating one another, the principals climbed into the city's Chrysler and, headed by the Chief on his Harley, the entourage sped off. Deputy Wright took down the barricade, gave me a goodbye wave, and I was alone.

I walked a few paces to the north, listened, and walked back to the south. I listened again, but I heard nothing. I knelt, and with my face six inches from the concrete, I looked, but I saw nothing.

During the next several days, the interstate remained inert, but Joanna suddenly sparkled.

More from boredom than from a sense of duty, she had volunteered to man the patient information desk at Mt. Hope Confederate Memorial. At first, it was only two hours on Thursday; then came the sparkle, and soon it was four on Thursday and two on Friday morning; not long after, it was eight hours nearly every day. Joanna put on eye shadow with extra care—she who had always worn less makeup than Pete Seeger—and bubbled from the dressing table, "Dr. Hollingsworth is such a dedicated physician, and the nurses adore him."

It wasn't long before Dr. Hollingsworth was Rip. That he was the son of President Hollingsworth contributed to the change. That he was, at twenty-seven, only three years younger than Joanna and looked, and dressed, and played like a young Arnold Parker contributed even more.

And then one day, the sparkle had a tear.

It was Friday night, and we were taking Denise—the maid Joanna had recently hired to do the housework—to her home in the Quarters. At Lincoln High, newly built to replace the one the interstate ate, we saw a small group surrounded by mounted state troopers. I slowed, but Denise said from the back, "Don't you stop, Mister Doc. There ain't nothing there but trouble."

We dropped Denise off at her place, but on our way back, Joanna said, "Look."

The group was milling around the school steps. Some were unloading sleeping bags from a Volkswagen van, and others were carrying the bags and packs into the buiding.

"I know him!" cried Joanna. She pointed at the one white man with the group. "I know him!"

She jumped out, almost before I could stop, and waved. "Joanna!" he saw her, and she raced into his arms.

"Keith, this is my husband." I looked my age and he looked surprised, but we shook hands.

"Keith and I were arrested in New Orleans," Joanna giggled.

"Jailbirds," Keith grinned back. "Hardened criminals."

Joanna barely suppressed another giggle, "What's happening?"

"We're marching to Baton Rouge to protest job discrimination. Here, let me introduce you to Rap."

Keith led us to a small, wiry man in dark glasses. "Rap, this is Joanna. Joanna and I were two of the McCory Five."

Even behind his shades, I saw Rap's eyes on Joanna go up and over each curve. He saw all he wanted to see and walked off.

"It's been a long day," Keith hastened to explain. "Long and in the 90s. And the horses kept crowding us. And," Keith paused, "since Memphis, it's been hard. Montgomery, Selma, Washington," he recited the achievements, "but now," Keith's voice rose and sank back. "Now it's as if the bullet that killed King killed the Movement."

"What you need is a martini, a bath, and a Joanna supper." Keith hesitated.

"We'd be pleased to have you," I assured him.

"Let me check with Rap." And we walked to where the march leader stood, his face considering the road his people had walked that long, hot day.

In her best, liberal, Unitarian, rich-side-of-Dallas voice, Joanna spoke, "I am going to steal Keith from you." And in a quick afterthought, "Won't you come too?"

Rap went over the curves even more deliberately and judgment complete, turned to watch the last trooper leave, his horse breaking into a jaunty, tail-swishing trot.

"No!" We heard the clipped word barely escape the tight lips.

That night, after the martini, the bath, and the supper, and after the two had recaptured the night they spent in the New Orleans jail under the not so gentle surveillance of Billowing Bill, the jailer—the two had so baptized because of his girth—I asked Keith, "Where did y'all start?"

His spirits restored, Keith retraced, how the week before, the march had journeyed west through Bayougoula, Cadiz, and Tours. It was the trail the Choctaw took on their way to trade with the

Natchez, the route de Soto might have walked, certainly the one traveled by LaSalle's lieutenants, and the same road the West Florida Republic had marched to carry the flag of independence to Baton Rouge: A path of meaning, a strip of history, a journey of time, embedded in the land.

The next morning on the porch we watched the sun rise over the interstate. On this Sunday, the superhighway lay empty across the land, more sterile than usual. Keith rose to go. I put my arm around Joanna and, longing to restore a precious moment so I might be with her, said, "Let's march."

Her body stiffened. In my longing, I had said the wrong thing. But with Keith watching, her only response had to be, "Let's do."

At Lincoln High, the troopers were back and in good spirits. The horses, catching the enthusiasm, joined in, and with arched necks, they swished, stamped, and occasionally nudged a nervous marcher carrying his pack roll to the Volkswagen.

Waiting in the front, I noticed cracks already zigzagging across the school's foundation. Woodard Fabrications had got the contract for the new structure—not surprising since the founder was on the school board—and when he poured the footing, Bubba had been overly generous with the sand.

Rap appeared, shades in place. Hoping to cross the distance, I walked over, and for the second time said the wrong thing.

"OK if we join you colored folk?"

"We black, man. We black," Rap stuck out a lightly tanned arm. "See!"

We looked at one another, him behind his dark glasses, and me behind my misspent intentions. But something warmer than a sneer crept across his face, and he shrugged, "If you want."

About fifteen of us walked through the Quarters to Main. Mt. Hope was on the edge of Klan country, and the more prudent members had left in cars for Baton Rouge during the night. At Main, policemen in helmets and night sticks, assigned by Mayor Gates "to protect" us, lined the street. Chief Gilmore swung his Harley around to the front, dismounted, plugged in his bullhorn, and announced, "You neegros, listen. Mt. Hope is a nice, Christian town, and I aim to keep it that way. You step out of line, and I'll put your ass in my jail and forget where I hung the key."

Amid the applause from the fast-gathering, church-dressed crowd, Gilmore mounted the Harley, thrust his arm forward, and shouted in his best Rawhide voice, "Move 'em out."

We had passed Edelstein's Jewelry and were only two blocks from the courthouse when the first cherry bomb arched from the crowd to explode at our feet. Its "POW" startled the policemen, but the seasoned troopers doffed their hats and spurred their horses into a prance.

Overhead, the vacant interstate cast a dark shadow about us. The noise of the march, the crack of the Harley, the ring of hooves, the thud of boots, and the shuffle of steps—sounds of the human struggle—reverberated against the emptiness that hung above us.

The second cherry bomb, accompanied by a shower of eggs, came as we passed Sillman's Drugs, a place where Mr. Sillman, a kindly man with gray hair and wire-rimmed glasses served cherry cokes and banana splits across a marble counter to teenagers twirling idly on anchored stools—but only, even in 1969, to whites.

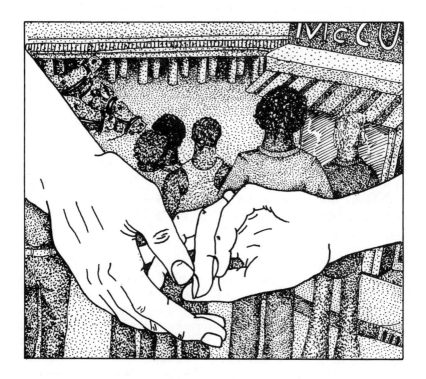

Near the center of town, we marched by McCory's, and suddenly Denise, her two hundred pounds splendid in purple leotards, was beside us. Joanna reached over for her hand and then across to mine, and I did the same for Keith. Together, we sang softly, almost privately, as if for us alone, the worn words, still beautiful,

Oh, deep in my heart,
I do believe,
We shall overcome someday.

On West Main, guarding the exit out of town, rose the Mt. Hope Confederate Memorial. Across the meticulous lawns, its white columns and classical pediment gleamed at us. Near the entrance, in the slot reserved for physicians, was Dr. Robert Hollingsworth's brilliant red Ferrari. Joanna's hand lay secure in my grasp, but I heard the tear as it fell.

That night Joanna loved me the way I had taught her, and she engulfed me until with a cry of "Mamma" I disappeared inside her.

The next morning, she spoke, "I remember Selma. But Keith's right. It's not there anymore." Afraid, scarcely daring, I looked. I looked, but in her eyes, I saw nothing, neither tear nor sparkle. My God, what had I done to her.

"Don't look so sad," she fussed. "I'm all right."

I went to the back porch and shook my fist at what crossed the pecan grove.

"You can't hide forever in your emptiness. You will, I tell you, you will be."

As soon as it opened, I was in the library at the card catalog. Under *I* for Interstate, I found only engineering specifications. Recalling the cracks at Lincoln High, I thought, "Ought to give those to Bubba." But under *H* for Highways, I found one entry after another. I checked out an armful, and panting from both the weight and the heat, I hurried to my office.

I shoved aside the nearly completed manuscript on witchcraft in Nueva Esperanza and began extracting notes. Some were upbeat: "These high speed, multi-lane, vehicular arteries funnel the nation's lifeblood from heartland to coastland." Some were critical: "From sea to shining sea, we are choking in a concrete straight jacket." Some were aesthetic: "The expressway has become a major art form of the contemporary world." Some were sardonic: "Superhighways are the greatest monument to death since the Pyramids." Some were philosophical: "To be on the interstate is to be suspended from reality." And one was peculiar: "In love with freeways, I go all the way with each I travel."

I considered the peculiar one that night as I poured Joanna her Chivas Regal and me my drugstore bourbon.

"I was curious as to what he might say," Joanna was speaking.

"Dr. Hollingsworth?" I knew better than to ask.

"Rip," she corrected. "As busy as he was, he took time to stop and say, 'How brave you were.'"

"Is that all?"

"Isn't that enough?"

"Well, yes, I guess so. Sure. You were brave." But what, the thought sneaked in, what of Keith? of Rap? of Denise? What of black and white together?

After supper, and for the first time, I crossed the pecan grove to the emptiness. I peered through the chain link fence. "Why did they build a fence?" I climbed up and jumped down to the other side. "What do they fear?" I put my hand out, gently, like a friend, or even more. I stroked and saw my strokes turned into caresses. I laid my forehead against the coolness, its coolness, the coolness of it inside, the it that I swore would be.

The next evening Joanna greeted me with a kiss, and I wondered why. I fixed the drinks and in the middle of Eric Sevareid's interpretation of Woodstock, she announced, "I received a letter from my father today."

"Oh."

"He implied he would consider a loan toward the purchase of my house."

My thoughts already on the it beyond the chain link fence, I replied, "I kinda like the one we are in."

The fight lasted through the news, through supper, and extended into the bedroom where Joanna's hand shook as she coated her tears with eye shadow.

"The Mt. Hope Confederate Memorial and Dr. Robert Hollingsworth both appreciated your dedication, particularly 'Rip,'" I commended her rigid figure. She paraded out the front, and I stamped out the back.

Humming Merle Haggard's "Lonesome Fugitive," I skipped through the trees and sang aloud Hank's "The Lost Highway," as I paused atop the fence.

"I could put it in a story."

I climbed down and strode toward it. "But it is not in a story. It is here, right in front of me." I placed my ear against it and heard it hum. "It's here, and it's alive."

Late that night, alone in bed, I considered, "If it is alive, it must have a name. I-8 is the name of a robot, not of a being who lives."

The next morning I didn't bother to make Joanna's tea, and left her still asleep. At my desk, I reviewed for the last time my account of witchcraft in Nueva Esperanza.

Nueva Esperanza, a town built and christened La Nueva Esperanza de la Santísima Madre by the Franciscans on their missionizing journey through northern Mexico, had only one witch, but she was large enough for all, including the anthropologist. People in Nueva Esperanza, products of malnutrition and intestinal parasites, were small, almost tiny, particulary the men. The witch, however, was strikingly robust and taller than Joanna, nearly as tall as me. Eyes, both male and female, glittered as she strode across the plaza, red roses pinned to her dark hair, rich laughter peeling from her wide lips, and a husband scurrying to keep pace. In the land of small bodies and smaller souls, she was La Comilona, the eater, the devourer, who feasted on the blood of male babies so that in the morning mothers found them withered and thin.

Strangely, Joanna, who was already finding in Nueva Esperanza what she would later discover all too soon in Mt. Hope, caught in La Comilona a response missing in the others, and the two spent so much time together whispers hinted they were sisters.

I asked Joanna that night as a peace offering, "Do you remember La Comilona?"

Instead of peace, she hurled back, "I called Father."

"So," I retaliated.

"So, I am leaving for Dallas tomorrow."

"Have a good trip!" I slammed the back door.

I climbed the fence as if the chain links were steps into a room, a bedroom. Inside, I ran my hands over its cool smoothness. "It's a she," I murmured in disbelief. "How could that be? A monster of concrete and steel, a she? The eater of miles and miles of trees; the predator of schools and churches, a she?"

The next day I brought flowers home to an empty house. On the porch were the remains of Joanna's late breakfast of nibbled toast and brown tea. I collected the delicate porcelain in hands more suited for the plow or the hoe, the same hands that broke pencils and bent typewriter keys. At the sink, afraid of what might happen, I washed each piece gently and carefully placed it on the drying rack. When I got to Joanna's cup, I cradled its fragile smoothness between my wet hands and raised it as if in offering.

"Loan, hell. He'll give her the money the way he gave her this tea service. And then what will I do? Tell them both to take their money and shove it? Or be nice and give in? Give in and give up. I guess it depends on how much I love her."

I put the cup down next to its companion saucer. From a cupboard I took a bottle of K&B's finest, gathered up the flowers, and went out on the porch. I poured the bourbon with one hand, and with the other still around the flowers, I watched the shadows in the pecan grove lengthen.

The first time I had seen her, really looked at her, was on the archery range at Sophie Newcomb College. Her face was complex. It was well-groomed and haughty when it appeared in the sorority section of the *Hullabaloo* where she and her Phi Mu sisters played court to the Homecoming Queen; it was contorted and angry when it appeared in the *Times-Picayune*, leading little black girls in ribbons past a shouting mob. On the archery range, it was different again.

Having just turned forty, I never missed an opportunity to walk by the range each Tuesday afternoon on the way to my room on Lower Line. Some girls were square and chunky, others thin and pimply, but she, a senior, was tall, sturdy, and not a blemish on that ivory-smooth skin. Dressed in a white tunic, her red hair pinned high and held by a blue ribbon, she pierced the bull's-eye with calm dispatch. With bow stretched, arrow straight, arm steady, she was, in 1960, the huntress, Joanna.

Now, six years after the death of John F. Kennedy, one year and four months after the death of Martin Luther King, Jr., and one year and two months after the death of Robert F. Kennedy, now, in 1969, was she still the predator? Or was she—empty of both sparkle and tear, sterile and without child—now the victim?

The pecan grove was dark when I climbed the chain links and entered the bedroom. I took off my shirt and laid the flowers around us. Even in the August heat, her skin was cool, cool and smooth, like ivory. I brushed my bare chest against her and felt my self harden. I reached for my belt and was naked. Empty, she waited to be filled, filled the only way a man can fill a woman. She, La Comilona de Millas, the Miles-Eater.

NOTE

1. Earlier version published *Amelia* 4, 1987: (68–87).

❦

THE MUSEUM[1]

I slammed the truck door shut, paused to watch the early Sunday sun flicker at the tops of the live oaks, and then walked from the faculty parking lot across the campus to the museum. Last night the first autumn front came through and broke the suffocating grip of the long, hot, Louisiana summer.

"It's great to be alive," I thought suddenly, and paused again to watch the morning come up. "Even for an old, retired codger like me." I started walking again. "Old farts can still feel."

Each weekend I opened the museum. I liked to get there early, long before the 10:00 A.M. opening time. Margaret said I must love the place because I spent more time there than I did at home.

"I have never understood why you want to be there every Sunday with all those dead things," she complained.

I replied, "We fossils have to stick together."

I'd rather tell her that, even if it made her mad, than to try to explain. It was just that I had built the museum, or the better part of it, and I liked to be with the things that I had built; they were a part of me, part of the museum world and me.

As usual, the lock in the big entrance doors stuck, and I fiddled with the key, pushing it in and pulling it back out, until I found the spot where the key and the lock became friendly and decided to let me in. I locked the doors behind me and turned to walk across the foyer into the main hall. From the east end, where the universe was exploding and the earth coagulating, I walked past the trilobites scuttling about on the floor of Cambrian seas, past the plants marching in ecological succession across the earth, past lung fishes panting in the thick Devonian air, on past carnivorous amphibians preying on Carboniferous insects, and then to the middle of the great hall and the section on reptiles. Here I stopped, as I nearly always did, to pay my respects to George.

George was a reptile man, a dredger of the Mesozoic. He was head of the zoo department when I first came, and a powerful man on campus. George was powerful not so much because of his scholarship—although early in his career he had stumbled across a new species of *Stegosaurus* in the Texas Cretaceous and promptly gave it the name *christianides*, in honor, he explained, of his father—but he was powerful because of his single-minded dedication to making everybody, chancellors included, do what George wanted done.

I soon discovered that if I could convince George that he wanted what I wanted, I'd be in good shape. So I convinced him he wanted a museum.

I wanted a museum so people could see the past. George wanted it so they could see him, as reincarnated in his *christianides*. So it was a workable arrangement.

George got the bottom floor of the new Natural Science building, and I drew up the plans, careful to put the Mesozoic and *S. christianides* in the center. I wangled money for material and in return George let me have the small room at the west end of the hall for prehistory.

"I wish I could let you have more, Miles," George said, leaning back in his swivel chair and gesturing at the plans laid out on his huge desk. "But when you consider the time span we're dealing with, beginning with the origin of the universe," he leaned forward to stab a thick finger in the direction of the east entrance. Then dragging it across the plans and stopping at the alcove at the west, he pronounced, "Prehistory, and especially Louisiana's prehistory, is pretty small potatoes."

"Sure," I shrugged, glad to get what I could for the past.

To stretch the funds, I made the displays myself. All one summer, the summer before the Korean War, Jim, my only graduate student, and I sawed, trimmed, and fitted. Even in the late forties, Louisiana was cypress-rich, and every cabinet Jim and I built was made of that warm, beautiful wood.

"Doc," Jim called one day and held up a particularly sensuous plank, one straight from the cypress heart and rippling with alternating rays of gold. "Doc," Jim stroked the plank, "it's so damn pretty, I could fuck it."

I touched the plank, and its soft glow warmed my fingers. "Too good for dinosaurs, that's for sure." The best cabinet we made that summer came from that plank, and when we finished, George wanted the cabinets painted a dark green.

"George, if you want 'em green, we'll paint the son of a bitches green as a gourd. But this one," I touched Jim's love, "this one, this one belongs to prehistory, so keep your cotton-picking hands off."

George, who was from Newark, New Jersey and had never seen cotton, much less picked it, didn't like what I said, but the last thing

Jim and I did that summer was to move the cabinet, unpainted, to the west end, ready to present the past.

I stood in the middle of the hall for a minute longer, looking at *S. christianides.* Six months after he retired, cancer got George. The last time I saw him, on his bed at Our Blessed Lady's, he was nothing but a skeleton.

I turned away from the exhibit and continued toward the west end. Off to my left, Archaeopteryx flew out of his reptilian heritage toward modern birds. To my right, the early mammals were likewise evolving, from egg layers to true mammals, whose young emerged from their mother's womb, alive and hungry for the breast, and then from tiny insectivores to the giants of the Ice Age. At the end of the hall, a mastodon raised its enormous tusks to trumpet my appearance. I walked under the tusks and stood beneath the sign, "Prehistory." Once more, as I had on a thousand and more weekends, I approached the past. I entered the place where I was.

The exhibits in the room, arranged, with one exception, chronologically, narrated the theme, "The Epic of the Louisiana Indian." Unlike Dr. Tanner-Fisher, my brilliant successor with a Berkeley doctorate and a husband in tow, who preached that archaeology was a hypothetico-deductive science, I believed that arrowheads and potsherds told a story.

Chapter 1 was a diorama on Indian life at the close of the Ice Age. In it, tiny figures were hurling spears at a huge bison stuck in a mud flat. The narration continued with scenes of how Indians feasted on Louisiana's abundant shellfish, on how others, farther north, first heard the secret of agriculture, and how later, others, influenced by the great cultures of Mexico, built temples on top of earthen mounds to beg from the gods an explanation as to why they were here. The final chapter was an exhibit on how all that millennia of effort, all the hunting and feasting, all the cultivating and the questioning, ended with the arrival of the whites, first de Soto and disease and then LaSalle and guns.

In the center of the room and out of chronological sequence, because there is a little George in us all, was my St. Marie material, displayed in a cabinet of unpainted, golden cypress. As I had done with George, I went to the cabinet to pay my respects to Jim.

Jim had found his first projectile point when he was a kid deer hunting with his dad, and by the time he came to the University he had a huge collection of what he called "bird points." He never got much beyond that stage in his archaeology, and in all honesty, Jim wasn't much of a student. He had trouble being serious. After he read that George's *Stegosaurus christianides* was an armor-plated giant with the brain the size of a walnut, he observed, far too loudly, "Like father, like son." But I liked Jim. I liked him a lot.

After a midterm of *C*s and *D*s, Jim came to the museum and found me finishing the St. Marie exhibit. We talked a bit, but not enough, not nearly enough. He was going to drop out, he explained, fondling the cypress cabinet, running his hand over it, lightly caressing the corners, going to drop out and join the Marines.

He gave the cabinet one last pat, and said, "I guess that's it."

"I guess so," I replied, not knowing what else to say. We shook hands and he left.

That summer the Korean War started. Jim was part of the landing at Inchon, which the experts immediately hailed as another shining star in MacArthur's already brilliant crown, but Jim never made it to the beach. They didn't even find his body until a week later. By then the sea creatures had taken away his face, and his skull had begun to bleach.

The cypress that Jim loved had become even more glowing through the years, and now it formed a halo around the St. Marie material. Inside the case, enshrined by the cypress, was my *Stegosaurus christianides*.

St. Marie was a major site, a hundred miles north of Baton Rouge, on the levee of the French Fork Bayou, near the tiny settlement of St. Marie. It was, or had been before we excavated it, a mound, the largest in the state and rivaling in size other major sites in the southeast, Moundville in Alabama, or Etowah in Georgia. There may have been other mounds in the area, but one hundred fifty years of plowing and harrowing had leveled them. In fact, we dug the St. Marie mound because the landowner, a cotton planter, wanted it out of the way.

"Y'all better come and dig that thing 'cause I'm going to tractor it down."

With that threat to obliterate the past hanging over our heads, we contacted the WPA regional office in Memphis, made what plans we could, and left for the field in the early summer of 1938.

I was the field supervisor, and my immediate bosses were two Ivy League Ph.D.s. The Ph.D.s ran the lab in Baton Rouge, and I dug the mound. We had a shovel crew of fifty men, thrown out of work by the Great Depression and eager to earn the little we could pay them. The first thing we did when we got to St. Marie, even though it was long past supper time, was to go out to the site.

The mound rose from the surrounding fields and thrust upward nearly fifty feet. The slopes were covered with second growth sweet gum, but at the peak was a red oak, so tall and thick that it seemed to join the sky with the earth.

As we looked up at the mound, Tig, an illiterate sharecropper from the Mississippi Delta but, thanks to Roosevelt's WPA, a veteran of digs up and down the lower valley, and now my foreman, remarked, "She's a big 'un."

"The first thing to do," I answered, "is to clear her off."

Tig nodded, but added, "Seems a shame."

I wondered about that too, as we watched the night's mantle cover the mound. Even in the dark, we felt life around us, a stirring at our feet, a sighing overhead, a cough farther up.

The crew worked hard, and a week later, Tig announced, "She's naked."

Denuded of her cover of trees and laced with five foot squares I had laid out, the mound was ready. Even with the first shovels, she offered up the past: pottery with bold, incised designs, expertly chipped points with barbed bases for hafting; thick, ground stone adzes; tobacco pipes with effigy bowls; and ear spools made from copper. And then as we peeled off the first layer, we exposed the burials.

The mound had over a thousand, some children, but mostly adults; many with their legs drawn up to their chins, like embryos in a womb. As soon as the shovel struck one, work stopped, and everybody, Ph.D. and shovel hand, gathered around me. With trowel and brush, I gently brought the figure into view: the feet, the legs, the pelvis, the ribs, the arms, and the head.

Each time I flicked the last bits of dirt from the eyes, I wanted to lean over and whisper, "Hello. My name is Miles. Don't worry. We'll take care of you."

But I never did, and it's just as well. After photographs were taken, I tried to lift the skeleton from its earthen womb, and nearly every time, the skeleton disintegrated, leaving only a few white teeth and a fine powder barely distinguishable from the brown earth beneath it. At the end of the season, and out of the one thousand and more burials, we had only twenty reasonably intact ones. The Ph.D.s took them east, but soon bigger and better career opportunities called, and the Indian skeletons from St. Marie, Louisiana, were stored away and then lost among Egyptian mummies, South American shrunken heads, and New Guinea cannibal trophies.

Otherwise, the excavation was a success. It gave work to those who needed it. It launched the Ph.D.s on their illustrious careers. It got me my dissertation. And it established a Hopewellian pre-

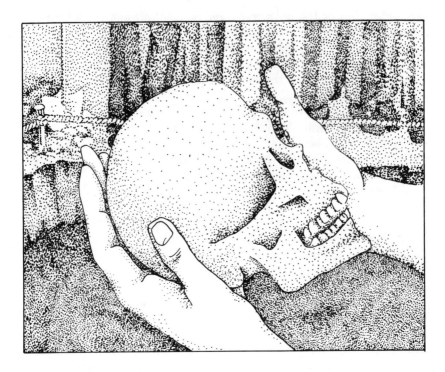

sence in Louisiana: the pottery designs, the effigy bowls, the copper ear ornaments, but especially the mound itself, told of a restless people who spread their vigorous celebration of death from their home in Ohio throughout much of eastern America and, now, thanks to St. Marie, as far south as Louisiana. It did all this because we loved our work. With our love we brought the past back and made it live.

It lived still today. It lived with me. Here in the museum.

I looked at the past, enshrined in its golden cypress case. Photographs retold the story of the excavation: the mound covered with sweet gum and impregnated with the red oak, the mound stripped and prepared for the shovel, and then opened, its children exposed, photographed, and carried off.

There were photos of the crew, of the Ph.D.s, of Tig and me. The ones of Tig and me showed us standing on top of the mound shortly after the start of the excavation and then one taken at the end, with the mound flattened. In the background of the last photograph was a small group of men and women huddled together staring across the smoothed surface at the photographer. I remembered asking Tig about them. "Injuns," he replied. I looked at them curiously. "Choctaw," he added. Seeing here and there a whiter face with blonde hair, I added with a know-it-all grin, "Bleached Choctaw," But Tig didn't reply. Instead, in a voice suddenly tired, he said, "Boss, we done what we came to do. Can't we go now?" And that was the last time I saw Tig. Today, was he somewhere like me? Living close to the past? Waiting for the last door to open so he could cross over and be in it?

Time to open the museum, the present past, the living past, and let others in, if only for a time.

I walked back to the entrance, swung open the huge doors, and there they were.

Oh, shit. Trouble with a capital *T.*

There were two, the younger one and an older man. The younger one stared at me, and I stared back. Centered above his dark face was a black hat with a flat brim. A yellow hat band with red thunderbird designs circled the round crown. The same thunderbird designs covered a black vest lined with silver buttons. A belt with a silver buckle held up his tight jeans, and on his feet were, I swear, moccasins.

He had been here before, harassing me with his impossible demands. "We want it all," he had shouted then, circling about the St. Marie exhibit, pounding on the case, sticking his finger in my face. "It's ours."

"Who in God's green earth are you?" I asked, not yet mad, but getting that way fast. "And stop pounding on the case."

"I'll tell you who we are," and he hit the case again, shaking the contents. "We are the true owners of the land. No," he corrected himself. "No, we do not own the land. The land owns us. The land brought us forth. Our tribal legends tell us that on that spot the Earth Mother, loved by the Sky Father, gave birth to us. There." And he pointed toward the photographs of the St. Marie mound. "We are the St. Marie Choctaw," he concluded triumphantly, and added, "We want it all back."

I tried to reason with him. I explained about the age of the St. Marie mound and how it was there long before the Choctaw moved into Louisiana. He was not impressed. "How do you know that?"

I walked over to the chart, "How Archaeologists Tell Time," and launched into my standard lecture on radiometric dating, but he stayed where he was and sneered, "You scientists. You measure time with chemicals." He planted his feet apart, raised his arms and tilted his head back. "We Indians live it."

With his feet apart and head back, he shook his arms. "For us, time is alive. We are joined by it to the land. Through the umbilical cord of time, the Earth Mother nourishes us." He lowered his arms, doubled a fist, and waved it at me. "Pollute time with chemicals and you kill the Earth Mother." He slammed his clenched fist down on the cabinet.

"Stop hitting that cabinet, damn it. And what's this Earth Mother crap?"

Ignoring me, he went on, "We and the land are one. What you dug up is ours. We want it returned to us." Again he hit the St. Marie exhibit.

"We particularly demand the return of the remains of our sacred ancestors. We shall rebury them so that they may rest once more in the bosom of their holy mother. We also demand," and here his voice became strangely matter of fact, "all the money you collect from people who come here. You put us on exhibit and charge a fee. 'Step right up folks.'" His voice now thick with sarcasm. "'Step right up and see the dead Indian. That's a good Indian, folks. Yes, sir, that's a genuine, good Indian.' We want it all back, scientist. The objects, the bones, and the money."

His arm, swinging in a wide arc, hit the cypress cabinet the hardest blow yet. The top shelf slipped from its brackets, and photographs, pottery sherds, barbed points, and copper ear spools went crashing down. Startled by the disaster happening inside the case, the young Indian made as if to catch the falling objects through the glass walls. His fumbling simply knocked more off, but before I could tell him to get the hell away, he gave me one last hard look and left.

Now here he was again, in his garb, and with company too.

"My name is Hightower," the old man said and reached out his hand. "I apologize for my son's behavior. I taught him better than that."

The man wore what I would have worn if I hadn't become an anthropologist: a white dress shirt opened at the collar with the cuffs turned up, a pair of starched khaki pants, so stiff they cracked when he walked, and on his feet, polished brogans laced over white socks.

I took them past the *Stegosaurus*. "Reminds me of the Christians around St. Marie," the old man said with a polite smile, after hearing my explanation of George's namesake. But neither the dinosaur nor the mastodon interested him. When we entered prehistory, he headed straight for the St. Marie exhibit.

"Nice wood," his hands following the grain of the cypress. "Warm and soft, like a woman."

He listened patiently as I explained the excavation, the artifacts, and the photographs, which I had put back like they were

before the young Indian's assault. When I got to the last photo-graph, he interrupted.

"That's me." He pointed to a young, small figure at the edge of the huddled group staring across the flattened mound. "Everyday. All summer. You didn't see me, but I was there. Everyday. No one saw me. No one, except the foreman. Tig was his name. He saw me, but we never talked.

"Everyday I watched. I watched you cut down the trees, lay out the stakes, dig in the mound, and put what you found in paper bags. I watched you dig up our people, and being young, I wondered why the strong men of the settlement didn't stop you." The old man smiled at his youthful ignorance. "Later, I told my son, and he, being more foolish than me, came here to get our people. I see he was mistaken. You only have pictures. Where are the people?"

I recounted how the bones dissolved when we tried to pick them up, and as I spoke, I was once more back on the mound, brush-ing away the last bit of dirt, trying to speak the words of welcome, and then seeing the bones crumble into nothing.

"You dug up a thousand people, and this is all you have? Pictures? Pictures? Where are the people? Where are our fathers? Where are our the mothers? Where is our past?"

I replied that archaeologists dig up the past to preserve it, so others could see it.

The young Indian started to protest, but the older one shoved him aside and came close. For the first time, I saw his anger.

"It's ours. It belongs to us. Listen you, you white man. You took our land. You took our women. You even took our speech. But you can't take our past. It's ours. It stays with us. And until you kill us all, you cannot have it.

"Come on," the father said to the son. "Let us leave this place of death."

I got through the day. People came. I saw them go from one display to another. I saw them point out things. I saw them talk. The day was like that. I got through it. Closing time. At the door, I turned off the lights, first the Louisiana room, then the far half of the great hall, and then the part where I stood. The museum was dark. I put the key in the lock, and the bolt slid effortlessly into its slot. The sun was down. The night air was cool, even cold, and I shivered as I walked across the empty lot to the truck.

NOTE

1. Earlier version published in *The Southern Review* 20 1984: (919–927).

"GUG JJJUR"

Die Leute, die heute über die zwischenspezifische Nachright sprechen, wie die Psychologen, die Kenntnissingenieure, die Spezialisten der gekünstelten Intelligenz, und so weiter, solche Leute kennen ihre affenartigen Versuchskaninchen nur als Charaktere in einem zoologischen Lehrbuch oder in einem Laboratoriumsbericht.[1]

"In conclusion, those who engage in the disparagement of the linguistic capacity of the chimpanzee must now face up to our data set. We document, for the first time, language use in a triadic network of *Pan troglodytes-Homo sapiens-Pan troglodytes*. Furthermore, these data permit the generation of a nonhuman primate model of speech acquisition that tracks, in the most careful manner, the step-by-step process whereby language is acquired. Finally, the research reported here substantiates the effectiveness of the nonhuman primate model of speech acquisition in the improvement of language skills of those who, for reasons organic or environmental, lack the capacity for sustained interpersonal communication."

"Thank you, Dr. Boasz-Sauvage, for that most informative presentation. We are all in your debt. Dr. Boasz-Sauvage has just informed me that the Institute for Language Acquisition Research, directed by Dr. Francine Boasz-Sauvage and founded by Dr. Louis Sauvage, has recently secured additional funding from the National Institutes of Health to pursue the important work first initiated by Dr. Sauvage over thirty years ago. Francine, we are delighted.

"We will now hear a discussion of Dr. Boasz-Sauvage's paper by Dr. Charles D. Hooton. Dr. Hooton needs no introduction to those of us, psychologist or primatologist, in the field of communications systems. Suffice it to say that for nearly twenty years Dr. Hooton from his citadel at Florida State has applied the principles of ecological theory to naturally occurring communicative competence, first among the *Lemur catta* of Madagascar, the *Alouatta beelzebub* of Central America, and for the last ten years, *Pan troglodytes* of Africa. In this march up the phylogenetic scale, so to speak, from prosimian, to monkey, and to chimpanzee, Dr. Hooton has vigorously advanced the position that communications systems are subject to the same selective pressures that operate on morphology and consequently are pulled in the direction of Darwinian fitness. Dr. Hooton."

"What you have here is rehash. There's not a thing new. You take this so-called triadic network. Sauvage first told us he had chimps talking in his lab back in the late forties. Had a machine then too. A Chimp-O-Mat. He gave the chimp a number three washer—called it "money"—and the chimp put it into a slot, pushed a button with a banana painted on it. And presto. Out dropped a banana. Which the chimp ate—peeling and all.

"Only thing different you see here is the machine is smarter. You take a Chimp-O-Mat, put in a few options, find yourself an idiot to 'network' with two chimps trained like circus monkeys, and you have the 'data set' Francine is so proud of."[2]

"I must protest. Not only is Dr. Hooton's characterization of our work ludicrous but his term 'idiot' violates accepted cannons of scientific usage. Such gross appellation clearly reflects a prejudicial attitude, which frankly I'm not at all surprised to hear."

"Dr. Boasz-Sauvage, as a discussant, Dr. Hooton is entitled to an uninterrupted opportunity to present his assessment."

"And I am entitled to refute."

"Dr. Hooton."

"You also have here the error Louis began with. You also have here the blinders he put around his eyes. So he could see what he wanted. What he wanted was to see a chimp talk."

"What a terrible distortion of our research program."

"Please, Dr. Boasz-Sauvage."

"You have a refusal to approach chimpanzees as a naturally occurring species in the context of an ecologically tuned system. You have a refusal to consider chimps as chimps. Instead, you have two chimps, two male chimps, raised in diapers. And called, God knows why, Margaret and Ruth.

"You want it worse than he did, Francine. Whatever it is you want, you want it bad. What do you want them to say, Francine? 'Gimme banana' like that idiot?"

"Have you finished, Dr. Hooton?"

"For now."

"Very well. Dr. Boasz-Sauvage will have ten minutes in which to address the points raised."

"For years, Dr. Hooton has completely misunderstood the work of my husband. When I first came to the Institute in Atlanta on a post doctoral from Columbia, where I had completed my work on the effect of protein deprivation on the learning curve of *Rattus norvegicus albinus*, Louis had returned from a AAAS symposium similar to this and held here in Los Angeles. He told me he had gone to the meeting with the highest of hopes that if he explained to Dr. Hooton the true goal of the program, Dr. Hooton could not help but grasp its purpose. Instead, Dr. Hooton, as he has today, remained stubborn. So deeply wounded was my husband by Dr. Hooton's obstinate behavior that Dr. Sauvage abandoned all further attempts to dialogue with Dr. Hooton. The depression he suffered from the perverse resistance of Dr. Hooton contributed, I have no doubt, to my husband's illness—an illness which most unfortunately confines him to the Institute; an illness which has devolved upon me the impossible task of speaking for him.

"Lacking the idealism of my husband, I have no alternative but to disregard Dr. Hooton's intemperance. Instead, I will concentrate on you, the unbiased audience. With what you have already seen, I am confident that with additional exposition, you will perceive, in the manner Dr. Hooton is constitutionally incapable of, the aims, and the achievements, of the Institute.

"Let me state once more our goal. We propose to analyze the language learning process whereby the human infant progresses from random vocalization to the imitation of adult sounds to the functional transference of those sounds to verbal operants, or 'words,' and finally to the relational grouping of verbal operants into autoclitic processes, or 'syntax,' at which point the child may be said to possess language.

"While we agree with Skinner that verbal behavior, or more commonly, language, takes place in a learning mode,[3] and requires nothing more than adequate stimulation—certainly not anything as mysterious as an 'innate grammaticality'—we find the speed with which the human child moves through the later stages prohibitive for fine grain analysis. We use *Pan troglodytes* not to make them 'talk,' as Dr. Hooton so absurdly maintains, but because their learning proceeds at a slower rate.

"We recognize the language capabilities of the *Pan* species are limited, particularly with regard to vocalization. It is, however, *precisely* this limitation that permits us to construct a model that traces the acquiring of language from first sounds to 'syntax.'"

"Syntax, Francine? 'Gimme banana' syntax, or real syntax? Real syntax like 'I am a man' syntax?"

"May I be permitted to refute without harassment?"

"You may indeed. Dr. Hooton, please cooperate."

"Unfortunately, time constraints prohibit me from reviewing with you the long and distinguished history of the Institute. Suffice it to say that even before the Gardners, with whom my husband collaborated and whose contributions they continually ignore, popularized the strategy of bypassing *troglogytes'* limited vocal range, the Institute has sought to bridge the communication gap between the species through the medium of gesture rather than voice. Likewise, years before Rumbaugh developed the Yerkish lexigrams in the LANA project, Dr. Sauvage, through the creation of a visual lexicology, tapped the manual dexterity of the *Pan* species to achieve non-speech symbolic exchanges between *troglodytes* and *sapiens*. Contrary to Dr. Hooton's disparagement, the instrument my husband invented gave us all important first data on non-speech language. Subsequent developments have allowed the computer enhancement of the instrument." (See Appendix A, Fig. 2)[4]

"A Chimp-O-Mat by any other name is a Chimp-O-Mat."

"Please, Dr. Hooton."

"The non-speech alternative to *troglodytes-sapiens* communication has paved the way for the achievement of our final goal, the application of the nonhuman primate model of language learning to the improvement of the linguistic skills of the developmentally delayed. To assist these unfortunate subjects to express their innermost desires—and to respond to the instructions of others—is our ultimate aim."

"You get more grant money that way."

"Dr. Hooton, I must ask you to allow Dr. Boasz-Sauvage to continue."

"Thank you. Let me review with the audience evidence of the power of our nonhuman primate model as applied to the human case."

"Does everyone have a copy of the handouts? Dr. Hooton?"

"I don't need them."

Table 1

Subj	Sex	Chron Age	Stanf Binet	Lang Skills	
				Comprehension	Production
1	F	18 yrs	1 yr	Simple commands but only in context	Two words approximations
2	M	6 yrs	2 yrs	Simple commands	Imitates words; identifies body
3	M	15 yrs	5 yrs	3 yr equivalent	Severe dysarthria. Sounds not intelli. to native sp.

"Table 1 lists the attributes of subjects at the onset of their entrance into our program. Please note that all three have a Stanford-Binet age at great variance with their chronological age. At admission, all had subpar skills in comprehension and particularly in the production column. Case #3 had the highest in the comprehension category and had the greatest range of sound production. Because of a lingual dysfunction, however, his voicings were not discernible with regard to meaning and were, and in all likelihood still are, random articulations."

"And now, like a good Sauvage, he speaks perfect chimp."

"I'm going on to Table 2."

"Wait. Let's insure that everyone has Table 2. There are extra copies. Pass them to the back. Everyone has Table 2? There are extra copies."

Table 2

Subj	Yrs in Study	Lexipics	Sequencing
1	3	19	None
2	Dismissed after 10 months; behav danger to self and staff		
3	3 yrs & 2 mos	45	2 lexipics

"Table 2 lists the achievements of the subjects. After three years in our program, the first subject, a severely delayed case, showed considerable progress. By responding to the actemes designed by Dr. Sauvage and displayed on the Lexipic Viewer, she appropriately serialized the actemes necessary for communicating nineteen visual verbal operants. This is a remarkable achievement for such a handicapped person."

"About six 'words' per year."

"The third subject. . . ."

"What about case #2?"

"What?"

"The second subject. She? He? It? What happened?"

"Dr. Hooton, the table that Dr. Boasz-Sauvage has given us clearly explains that this subject was dismissed after ten months. The subject's behavior was a danger to him . . . her? . . . him, to himself and to the staff. It is not uncommon for human retardates to exhibit behavioral dysfunctions. In my own research, I have had to confine them."

"Put 'em in a cage like a mad dog?"

"Dr. Boasz-Sauvage, please proceed."

"The third subject is, if I may use that term, our star. In as far as we can ascertain, prior to his entrance over three years ago into our program, he had been institutionalized since childhood. His biocard gives little information on his parents and circumstances surrounding his institutionalization.[5]

"He had responded positively to the training and clearly enjoys interacting with Margaret and Ruth. During the sessions at the Operant Console, however, he tends to overexcite. This emotional peaking, which unfortunately has increased sharply of late, causes him to revert to the random vocalizations noted earlier. The behavior does impede his work with Margaret and Ruth. Prior to these outburst, he manifested an excellent performance pattern. I refer you to Table 2. The subject, case #3, reacted to the actemes on the Operant Console so as to communicate forty-five lexipics. Completely apart from his truly astonishing increase in vocabulary, he sequenced two lexipics to formulate a subject-initiated extended request.

"What's his name?"

"What?"

"What is his name? Case #3 has a name, doesn't he?"

"Yes."

"Well, what is it? François? No. Not François. Françoise. Françoise? Francine."

"His name is Miles."

"Not Françoise?"

"No."

"Does he have a last name? Most people have a last name. Does Case #3 have a last name?"

"Yes, of course."

"Well, what is it?"

"Dr. Hooton, Dr. Boasz-Sauvage has told you the retardate's name. May we go forward without further delay?"

"Thank you. At the beginning of his interaction with the Operant Console, Case #3 . . . Miles . . . encountered obstacles that matched those initially confronted by Margaret and Ruth. Likewise the procedures that proved successful for Margaret and Ruth assisted Case #3 in the mastering of these obstacles. This performance pattern we can credit to the nonhuman primate model. The centerpiece in the model is the request paradigm.

"I now turn your attention to the screen overhead. As part of the data collection strategy, we utilize the video camera extensively.

What you are now seeing is a segment, chosen from the many we have, of the request paradigm in action."

He was out of the place where he laid on the bed. She let him out. She came and talked her tongue at him. He could see talk. Her talk smiled her lips. Her talk wasn't a hurt. He could see. He could see talk.

The hairies were with the buttons. She talked her tongue at them. They pulled her clothes. They could pull clothes. They could pat. They patted, and she smiled her lips. He couldn't pat. He patted, and she shouted her tongue hard.

The hairies smelled dark. He didn't like the smell. It smelled dark. The dark he was locked into. The dark he was locked into back in the then. In the then when he was alone. He cried when he was locked alone. He cried in the dark, and the one they called mommy came and slapped him, and he did not now cry. He did not cry never.

The hairies barked. The big hairie made a tooth face. The little hairie made a tooth face. They barked. The big hairie climbed on her chair and screamed. The little hairie cried. She talked her tongue at the little hairie, and it stopped crying. The hairies smelled dark. He never now cried.

"In the request paradigm we proceed in a step-by-step fashion. Initially the request is made to the Operant Console. We permit the subjects . . . Margaret and Ruth, I mean . . . to watch us bait the site, usually with their favorite snack, M&M chocolates. They then directly address the Operant Console with the request for food. They must react to the individual actemes to organize a single visual verbal operant, a lexipic, if you please, and they must sequence the lexipics appropriately for the Operant Console to respond in turn. To illustrate, I refer you to the sheet titled 'A Simplified Guide to Operant Speech.'"

"I don't have that."

"It is with the tables."

"I don't have it."

"It's with the tables. Do you have the tables? You said you had the tables."

"It's not here. I don't have it."

"Dr. Hooton, please. Here, you may use mine."

"Why should I use yours? Besides, won't you need it, to speak operantly?"

"I would like to continue."

"I don't have a copy."

"Dr. Hooton, you must allow Francine, Dr. Boasz-Sauvage, to proceed."

"Without a copy, I may have to interrupt."

"Dr. Hooton. Dr. Boasz-Sauvage, please, let's go on."

A SIMPLIFIED GUIDE TO OPERANT SPEECH

Acteme		Lexipic	Functional Class
Pose	Pose'		

Behavioral Sequence

Operant Speech

English: *Give Margaret Ocie M&M.*

Free Translation: *Ocie, please give me M&Ms.*

"On the screen, Margaret, the larger subject, requests the Operant Console, Ocie, to give her . . . him . . . the candy. Please note that to make the request Margaret must not only sequence the lexipics, she . . . he . . . she . . . Margaret must embed in the request chain the correct response to the individual actemes. In this hierarchization, Margaret's behavior is much more language-like than the single level action of the Rumbaugh subject, Lana, and far more than that of the Gardners' Washoe. Next, in the request paradigm, and as we see here, Margaret requests Ruth to ask Ocie for M&Ms. Needless to say, the step from Request 1 to Request 2 is not accomplished without considerable training. More importantly, it requires that one subject anticipate the behavior of the other. Behaviorally, to anticipate, and I am quoting Bates here, 'is to be aware a priori of the effects a behavior will have upon the object, person or artifact, addressed.'[6] Such behavior Bates defines, and both Dr. Sauvage and I agree, as intentional communication. To intend an effect upon another is a fundamental property of speech.

"The next step, Ruth becomes the initiator and requests Margaret hand her . . . him . . . a tool, the hammer you see on the screen. Ruth, under the watchful eye of Margaret, hammers a peg. The hammering activates the Operant Console, which responds with a request of its own, to which Margaret replies. May I play through the hammering sequence again? As you watch, please note that hammering with its focused energy is not a natural gesture of the chimpanzee. It is a learned trait, and thus, in their hammering, Ruth and Margaret exhibit a capacity to acquire, in the proper environment, culture."

"What is the big chimp doing with that mirror?"

"The mirror belongs to an experiment designed to test the obtainment of a self-concept."

"Look, Francine. He is holding the mirror up to you. What do you see? Do you see yourself? With a hammer? Hammering a banana? What do you see, Francine? 'Mirror, mirror, on the wall, who is the monkey after all?'"

"I will proceed to the final step in the request paradigm, which is the integration of *Homo sapiens* into the network."

He wanted it right. She smiled her tongue. Her talk was soft. He wanted it right. She didn't smell dark. She smelled soft. She leaned her face close. He wanted to pat.

He hoped it was right. He worked on it all night. He didn't lay down in the place where the bed was. He stood. All night and practiced.

She smiled her tongue. He pushed a button. She smiled her tongue. She leaned her face. Her lips had a laugh. He pushed another button. One of the hairies push a button. She talked her tongue at the hairie. The hairie gave him the candy. The hairie smelled dark. The candy smelled dark.

She smiled her tongue. She leaned her face. Her lips had a laugh. The laugh was soft. It was close. He wanted to pat.

He wanted to get it right. He stood. All night and practiced. She leaned her face. Her lips had a laugh. The laugh touched his mouth. It tasted good. He wanted to pat.

"What is Case #3 doing, Francine?"

"He is just giving me a drawing. He draws continually. Compulsively. He goes through a pad in one day, and would use more if we provided it. He draws the same scene and accompanies the drawing with the same sounds. As with the vocalizations, however, the drawings are not discernible in terms of their content." (Ed. note. See Appendix B of this document.)

"No, he is talking. He is speaking to you, Francine. Turn it up so we can hear, Francine. What he is saying to you?"

"He is *not* speaking. He cannot speak. He is simply producing the vocalizations. He is in the emotional peaking. It interferes with his networking."

"He's speaking, Francine."

"He is *not* speaking. He cannot. But if you say so, then listen. Here."

"Jjjur. Jjjur. Gug Jjjur."[7]

"Did you understand, Dr. Hooton? I'll play it back, just for you."

"Jjjur. Jjjur. Gug Jjjur."

"Care to hear him again? Shall I turn up the volume?"

"Jjjur. Jjjur. Gug Jjjur."

"He's talking to you, not me."

"Is that talk, Chuck? Is that talk?"

"Jjjur. Jjjur. Gug Jjjur."

"Is that talk? Tell me, Chuck."

"Dr. Boasz-Sauvage. Dr. Hooton. On the behalf of those attending, we thank you. . . ."

"To repeat, the final step in the request paradigm is the integration of *Homo sapiens*, as both the initiator and recipient, into the interlexipic communications network. To review that step. . . ."

"Dr. Boasz-Sauvage, we are out of time."

"In conclusion, therefore, I repeat that those who disparage the linguistic capacity of *Pan troglodytes* now must face the data, available on video tape from the Institute to any legitimate researcher."

"Dr. Boasz-Sauvage. . . ."

"In conclusion, therefore, I insist, that in addition, the development of the nonhuman primate model of language learning marks a tremendous advance in our continuing efforts to enhance the skills of those unfortunates who cannot enjoy the full and uninhibited use of language—the dominant syndrome of our species."

"Dr. Boaz-Sauvage. . . ."

"Any idiot can say 'Gimme banana.'"

"Dr. Hooton. Francine, Charles, please. . . ."

NOTES

1. Those who speak today about interspecific communication, psychologists, information engineers, specialists in artificial intelligence, and the like, know their simian guinea pigs only as characters in a zoological textbook or in a laboratory report" (my translation). C. D. Hooton, "Sprechen Sie Schimpanse?" *Das Reich der Tiere* 30(1987):30–35.

2. The reference to Chimp-O-Mat is ambiguous. If Dr. Hooton implies Dr. Sauvage invented the Chimp-O-Mat, then either he or Dr. Sauvage is in error. J. B. Wolfe of Yale University, who pioneered the use of tokens in eliciting work-tasks in the 1930s, is the original developer of the food vender for chimpanzees. Cf. J.B. Wolfe, "Effectiveness of Token-Rewards for chimpanzees," *Comparative Psychological Monographs* 12(1936):1–72. See Appendix A (Fig. 1) of this text.

3. Dr. Boasz-Sauvage is no doubt referring to B. F. Skinner, *Verbal Behavior* (Englewood Cliffs, New Jersey: Prentice-Hall, 1957), whose theory asserts a child's linguistic development is determined by what we do to him. Consequently, the child's speech—and behavior in general—becomes a mirror image of our own.

4. In her eagerness to defend her husband, and thereby, perhaps, to draw attention to what she considers her own not immodest accomplishments, Dr. Boasz-Sauvage has made statements that appear exaggerated. Despite a "distinguished history," the Institute for Language Acquisition Research remains unlisted in the Directory of Scientific Organizations. On the other hand, a careful review of the writings of the psychologist couple R. Allen and Beatrice Gardner and those of the psychologist Duane Rumbaugh, who first used computers in chimpanzee language research, does, indeed, support her charge that neither the Gardners nor Rumbaugh have recognized Sauvage's investigations.

5. Subsequent research has disclosed this subject came from a background not unlike that of "Genie." See S. Curtiss, *Genie: A Sociolinguistic Study of a Modern-Day "Wild Child."* (New York: Academic Press, 1977).

6. The quote is at best a paraphrase. See p. 36, E. Bates, *The Emergence of Symbols.* (New York: Academic Press, 1976). It is curious that Dr. Boasz-Sauvage cites the Bates volume since Bates argues against a return to Skinnerian behaviorism, the very position Dr. Boasz-Sauvage advocates.

7. As with much of this text, "Gug Jjjur" is an equivocal utterance. One interpretation is that the vocalization is no more than a "subject-initiated extended request" that the experimenter respond affectionally. A second reading is "Gug Jjjur" is a plea, however gutteralized by the boy's twisted mouth and crippled self, a plea that Dr. Boasz-Sauvage give love and give it freely, lovingly, in the fullness of care, without the expectation of a reward, or as she might say, a reinforcer.

APPENDIX A

Figure 1. Cross-Sectional View of the Wolfe Vender

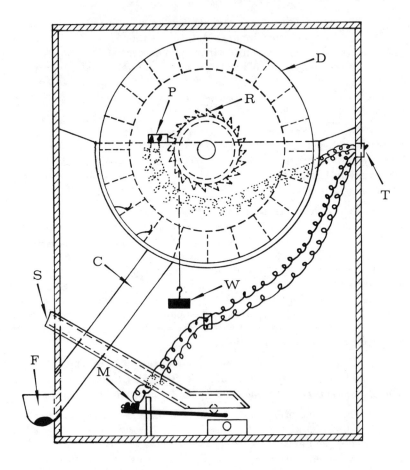

Key: D, Food Drum; R, Ratchet; P, Pawl; T, Toggle Switch; W, Weight; C, Chute; S, Token Slot; M, Trigger; F, Food Cup

Figure 2. Block Diagram of the Sauvage II, The Neo Chimp-O-Mat

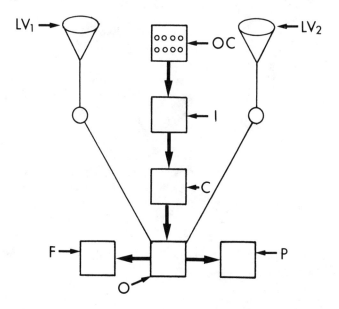

Key: LV₁ LV₂ Lexipic Viewers; OC, Operant Console; I, Imput Code; C, Computer; O, Output Signal; P, Print Out; F, Food Cup

APPENDIX B

Figure 3. The Art of Case #3

According to J. H. Di Leo, a Director of the Developmental Clinic, New York Foundling Hospital, and an authority on drawings by emotionally deprived children, the absence of arms in figures drawn by a child over 10 is an overt statement, "eloquent in its plaintive despair," of a crippling timidity. From this observation, we may infer that the figure to the extreme right, tottering on unsupportive feet, is a self-portrait. In Di Leo's view, heavy shading betrays anxiety over the organ shaded. Consequently, the facial protuberance, remarkably phallic, of the center figure is apparently a tongue. Even this brief note suggests that Dr. Boasz-Sauvage's dismissal of the drawing is premature, almost cavalier—an attitude others have attributed to her, one suspects with good reason. J. H. Di Leo, *Children's Drawings as Diagnostic Aids*, (New York: Brunner/Mazel, 1973); *Interpreting Children's Drawings*, (New York: Brunner/Mazel, 1983).

THE MAN-EATER

The only real reality is that found in *The Fourteenth Book of Bokonon.*

Kilgore Trout

. . . post-modern anthropology seeks to incarnate the transcendental object called LANGUAGE. . . .

Steven Tyler

I first became suspicious of words after a futile effort to communicate my thoughts. Scholarly thoughts, to speak frankly, easily become convoluted. Reflecting upon reflections and interpreting interpretations spin the best of us into ever faster, ever tightening, hermeneutical circles.

Spinning hermeneutically is rough enough, but unless we share each other's circles, and to share we must talk, what was a harmless circulatory motion becomes a *circulus vitiosus*, and as the Latin says, that's bad.

It happened one day my circle was circling so fast and tightening so tight I could scarcely breathe. Choking and coughing, I staggered into the office of a colleague and slumped down in front of a long table where he, an archaeologist, was sorting potsherds. I grabbed the table to slow the spinning, took several deep breaths, and with care and precision, explained to him that my research had opened a whole new world in which culture becomes nature and nature culture.

Like the good archaeologist he was, he continued sorting, putting little potsherds into big piles and big potsherds into little piles. He stopped, turned to me, and with a knowing and somewhat condescending smile, said, "Ponchartrain Checkstamp."

In return, I frowned, and suggested, again with care and precision, that on the other hand new worlds had a way of turning into blind alleys. He nodded, grinned enthusiastically, and added, "Tchefuncte Plain."

This time, with little care and less precision, I argued, that world and alleys aside, there were no atheists in foxholes. He leaned back, lit up his pipe, stared at the smoke curling up from the bowl, pointed the stem at me for emphasis, and smugly concluded, "Alexander Pinched."

Well, I didn't take that sitting down. Jumping to my feet, I demanded to know how many foxholes had he ever observed in atheists. As I stormed out of his office, I hurled back that if he ever pinched my wife's alexander, he'd get a fist in his face.

Once I calmed down, I realized that, like me, my colleague had been made the victim of words. They had snared him in a hermeneutic, and as his hermeneutic spun differently from mine, we could not touch, and since we could not touch, we could not share thoughts.

Words were in full revolt. Like the science fiction robot that turns on its maker, so words were rising up against their speakers. Through hardening their categories, words intended to condemn each of us to a solitary confinement that would spin forever hermeneutically.

Well, that might be their intent, but these were the upstarts up with which I would not put. I had my own intent. My intent was to render words useless, to talk without them. Furthermore, I knew where to start.

In the Caribbean island of San Lorenzo, one of the lesser of the Lesser Antilles, there was reported to be a religious movement, known locally as Bokononism, whose leader, Lionel Boyd Johnson, or Bokonon, as Johnson was pronounced in the island's pidgin, had compiled his meditations into some fourteen voluminous volumes referred to collectively as the *Books of Bokonon*. Johnson-Bokonon had cast these meditations into an oblique poetic form called the "calypso." Many of these calypsos appeared, annotated and explicated, in the only authoritative work on the island and the movement, *San Lorenzo: The Land, The History, and The People,* by Philip Castle, son of the great altruist, Julian Castle, the Albert Schweitzer, some say, of the New World.

Never published, the Castle book has since vanished. Fortunately, excerpts, including the calypsos, found their way into a manuscript written by a rather simpleminded man whose parents called him "John," but whom others called, mysteriously, "Jonah."

John's, or Jonah's, manuscript, *The Day the World Ended,* was not completed. The author apparently had frozen to death in a freak Caribbean ice storm. As luck would have it, the manuscript fell into the hands of a K. Vonnegut, Jr., who tried to pass the work off as one of his own, exactly as he had done earlier with the fantasy fiction of Kilgore Trout, but no one believed him; so he threw the manuscript into the garbage. A year later, my archaeological colleague, who was at that time deep into historical preservation, dug it up during an excavation of the city dump. Forbidden by his profession to analyze any artifact with writing on it, he sent the manuscript to the Human Relations Area Files, an anthropological organization dedicated to the study of truth, cross-culturally.

HRAF, of course, was delighted. The document, being both definitively obscure and obscurely definitive, met their rigorous criteria for inclusion. So they quickly coded the manuscript, photographed it, and sent the microfiche to participating libraries, one of which, surprisingly, given the size of the football stadium, was the university where I taught.

Fired with enthusiasm for my plan to talk without words, I raced across the campus toward the library. Even though it was a typical South Louisiana summer day, hot as hell and twice as humid, I shivered and my sweat turned cold. A book lay open on a bench, its pages freshly blanked, and tracks that only words could leave marked a trail from the bench to a nearby moss-strewed oak. Its leaves rattled menacingly.

"I don't have much time," I thought. "Already they are restless."

The library, the words' lair, reverberated with maniacal laughter, the sound hyenas make as they circle the cornered prey.

"Hurry. Hurry, Miles." I fumbled with the microfiche, quickly scanning the set on which were duplicated the calypsoic meditations of Bokonon, searching for the way to speak without speech. The viewer, sympathetic to the words' cause, was overheating, and the cards curled dark at the edges. I came to the last card, to the last volume, to the *Fourteenth Book* itself, the summary work. It had only one word, "Nothing," and even that disappeared in a puff of arid smoke.

"I must have missed something," I said. "Surely 'Nothing' is not the last word."

I pawed through the cards that contained the earlier volumes. Several were already so badly scorched I could barely read them, but then, through the smoke, seconds before the machine melted the film, I found it: Jonah's description of the Bokononist ritual of the *boko-maru*.

When they do the *boko-maru*, I read, the Bokononists break through the individual hermeneutic to substantiate an ineffable collectivity. To the rhythmic beat of the 23rd Calypso, Bokononists meet soul-to-soul by touching sole-to-sole.

Of course! That's it! How simple! How pure, if somewhat smelly. Of all the monkeys, only we walk erect. Furthermore, the fossil record is quite explicit. We walked before we talked. We strode before we spoke. So, the way to cut the ground from under the upstart words was to remove their support. Without the walking, there could be no talking. Without the talking, there could be no words. Without words, we would not be sealed off, hermeneutically. Instead, we, joined sole-to-sole, would be together, united, merged into one.

On the horizon of that new day loomed yet another possibility. Through the *boko-maru* method, humans might establish a meaningful relation with another member of our order. I had to confess, however, that going sole-to-sole with a chimp did nothing for me. On the other hand, *National Geographic* might consider funding one of my female graduate students. In the meantime, I would secure a grant from the Wenner-Gren Foundation for Anthropological Research, go to San Lorenzo, and seek out the Master. There, as Bokonon's disciple, I would sit, naturally, at his feet.

Now, the thickening smoke told me it was time to leave. The machine was about to self-destruct and, no doubt, wanted to take me along. I sprinted down the hallway, dodging bookcases upended by angered words, like Charlton Heston dodging toppling buildings in a disaster movie. Just in time, I got to the entrance. I hurdled the security gate and landed on my feet, right in the belly of a word.

An enormous word, the largest of its kind, had been lurking among the biblical concordances in "Ready Reference." At the instant I leaped, it rushed outside, opened its mouth, and in I plopped.

That's where I am now: inside the belly of a word, which is like being nowhere I have ever been. On the outside, words are rough and uneven. They go up and down a lot, like a *w*. Inside, however, they are smooth, spongy, and full of slime. When I try to walk, I sink up past my knees, and when I grab for support, my arms disappear up to the shoulders. About the only thing I can do is slither.

Words are, indeed, hollow and full of hot air, but the air is sugary sweet, so saccharine that the spongy walls ooze. A steady drip from the ceiling adds to the slime on the floor.

The light in the belly of a word is white, unexpectedly white, a blinding white, a white so intense that I burrow my head into the spongy, oozing walls, but the walls regurgitate me, and I'm back to slithering in the slime.

In my slitherings, I have established that I am not in an adverb. For that favor, I am extremely grateful. Adverbs are the worst of a bad lot. I've never met an adverb I didn't hate, immediately.

I have also ascertained that the word in which I am has none of the filth of a filthy word. On the contrary, I have never been, anywhere, so clean, but the cleanness is like the light, so intense, so unearthly, so celestial, it hurts.

The word in which I am contains all the magic of all the words.

It is the omni-magician, the word of words, and I shudder at the size of its trick.

"Stop it," I tell myself. "Do something. Don't lie there, slithering in the slime, like a tapeworm. Get on your feet and be a man. Be a man and walk."

But even as my thoughts take verbal form, the huge gut convulses to suck them from me, and my brain empties out its contents. The white light glows pink, and the ooze drips scarlet on an incarnate floor. The giant belly resounds with gurgles as it twists itself for the final event in its digestive cycle, and the famous exit of proud man, the two-legged carnivore, is celebrated not with a bang, nor even with a whimper, but with a low rumble, a gentle burp, and then, nothing.

DON'T CRY

The girl, reluctant to leave the cool bus for the hot, smelly night, stopped at the opened door. Earlier, she had stood inside the door of the theater and hoped for courage to step out of her movie world, where she had spent the day. Now she longed for even more courage. Flames from the giant vents of the refinery across the street turned her dark into harsh day. The street was littered with debris, discards from lives now safe. To her left was the bar filled with shadows cavorting in blue neon. To her right, on the corner, its broken "24 Hours a Day" sign flickering above dim interior, was the Laundromat. The bus driver, with his own appointments to keep, rattled the door, so she, tugging with a certain random despair at what might have been a sun dress, stepped down. Immediately, behind her began the familiar stalk of a man's step.

At the Laundromat, the girl slowed, and she saw the man's shadow, cast long and thin by the flames, move past her feet. The shadow, itself in some way strangely familiar, moved to her knees and climbed her waist, but when it mounted her shoulders and loomed ahead, she hurried toward the corner, tripping in her haste on the broken sidewalk. Turning the corner, she raced into the dark with her arms spread to welcome its concealing softness, her face as empty as ever.

At the upstairs apartment, which people told her was home, voices, one old and smooth and the other new and brittle, came at her from the single bedroom.

"There she is now. Rosie? Rosie? Where have you been?"

"Why do you worry, Mother? You know she has spent the day at the movies. The first in line and the last to leave. Whatever is showing. She lives on them."

"Rosie, here's your sister. She dropped by for a visit. Isn't that nice? Say hello to her."

She ignored the thin, silver-gray figures barely visible against the bed where one lay and the chair where the other sat. In a hurry to rid herself of its clinging sweat, she pulled at her dress. She hadn't liked the movie. It was one of those disaster films, about an earthquake in California. She could still see the earth yawning open to gulp down screaming people. Maybe there would be a different one tomorrow.

"Say hello, Rosie. Please."

Putting another tear in the dress already split under the arm and at the seams, she finally got it up over her square body and off. She threw it at the unmade bed crammed under an air-conditioner that groaned aloud at the unequal task of keeping the room cool. She felt sorry for it and at times, to let it rest, she turned it off. But when she did, the voices fussed.

"Miss High and Mighty. She is too important to say hello."

She picked up a faded black robe from the pile of crumpled dresses and dirty underwear at the foot of the bed, and went into the bathroom. The voices got stronger.

"Rosie keeps things to herself. She talks. Lots of times I've heard her. When she thinks she is alone."

"Why will she not talk to us? Do we mean so little?"

She flushed the toilet, watched the water swirl down, and came out. The voices, the younger one leading the way, retreated. The old one hesitated, and then, in its tired way, repeated, "Rosie, here's your sister. Doesn't she look nice in her new white suit and hat. Say hello. Did you wash your hands?"

"Oh, Mother, she is too old for that. She is an adult. When I was her age, I was already married, even if it was to a nerd. But every girl is entitled to one mistake. Paul, on the other hand? Thank God for Paul. Paul reminds me of Father."

The voices were thin, like the voices in the movie, but these voices smelled. The old one stank of sick. For as long as Rosie remembered, it had smelled that way, the dank odor of vomit, never the fresh sunlight of a new flower blooming. The other voice, the third voice, the father-voice? How had it smelled? The young voice smelled like a silly fly.

"One thing about Rosie. You do not have to worry about boys. Who would want a girl who never showed any feelings? Who never said 'I love you,' even if she didn't mean it."

The fly stopped but started again, and she wrinkled her nose at its buzzing.

"Look at her. What goes on in her head? You know, I have never seen Rosie cry. Not once. Not even that time she fell down the stairs and broke her arm. Not a tear."

"She just likes to keep to herself. She always has. When she was little, she'd get the chairs from the dining room—that's when we lived near Capital High where Peter taught and we had that lovely dining room with French windows—she'd get the chairs and make a circle. Inside the circle, she'd spend hours with her arms hugged around her knees, rocking back and forth, singing little songs to herself."

The father-voice? How had it smelled? Worse than sick.

"I remember. It was right after, right after the, the wreck."

"Yes, she was a little baby, barely able to walk. It was a miracle she survived."

"She would not have, if Father had not shielded her with his body."

The father-voice? She remembered now. It had the stench of nothing.

"Why, Mother? He was such a good man, my father. He died and Rosie lived. Why?"

She crisscrossed the space in front of the voices and was in the part called "kitchen" before they knew she was gone. The stubborn latch on the refrigerator's door at first refused to yield to her fumbling, but she hit it hard with her fist and yanked open the door. She thrust an arm past a plastic container of potato salad dark with fungus and grabbed a Coke by its thick neck. As she wrestled it out, the bottle slipped from her grasp and thudded against the floor. The voices were alarmed.

"Rosie?"

She pried open the Coke, and from its mouth, it spewed a brown mist over the dishes stacked to dry.

"Don't you dare mess up that kitchen. I just finished cleaning it. This place is awful. Dirty clothes everywhere. On the bed. On the dresser. And look at that pile on the floor. All Rosie has to do is to scoop them up and take them to that launderette on the corner. It will not hurt her."

"She hates going so much I usually do it. But this last week or so I simply haven't had the strength."

"So she hates doing a little work? She had rather live in squalor? Well, I do not like my mother living in filth."

"Rosie's a good girl."

She watched the drops of Coke form rivulets meandering down the plates to drip off the edges into puddles underneath the drying rack. She touched one of the puddles with a stubby finger and traced it into another puddle and another until she connected all the ones she could reach into a network of miniature lakes and rivers on the green landscape of the counter.

"Good-for-nothing is what Rosie is good for. The rest of us work. If she only had a job, you could move out of this horrible neighborhood and into a house like we had when Father was alive. Before Rosie was born."

She poured what was left of the Coke into a large glass, filled the glass with ice, and went back to the bedroom. The voices flashed on and off, as if they were afraid of her. Voices were so funny. She sat in front of the dresser mirror and watched the glass come up to her lips; she saw the ice cubes pile against her face. The cool, sweet liquid entered her mouth. She held it until her mouth nearly overflowed and then gave the Coke permission to slide past her throat and go slowly, so slowly, down into her stomach. Down, down, down. The voices were faint now, faint and far away. She couldn't even smell them.

"We're managing. Thanks to the help Paul and you give. That plus social security. We're managing."

"Yes, I know you are, and I wish we could help more. What makes me mad is not that Rosie does not have a job. I realize no one will hire her. But what makes me so mad is that Rosie acts as if we were not even here, as if we did not even exist."

"Don't be so hard on her. She's your sister."

"My sister? Look at her. Short, dumpy, dark, and hairy. Hairy legs, hairy armpits, and even a moustache. My God! My sister? No way."

The voices were so distant now they must be in another world, another galaxy, even another universe.

"I have to go, Mother. Paul will think I am still at Le Paris. Not that he would complain. He understands that a girl needs a break."

"Thank you for coming, and for doing the dishes. You're a good daughter. Rosie, say goodbye to your nice sister. Rosie?"

"Hello."

"Hello is it? Now that it is goodbye. A brilliant conversationalist. Do not bother, Mother. She is off in whatever world she lives in. Rosie? Do you ever stop at Le Paris? Free drinks for the ladies every Thursday. You should do that, Rosie. Go there and get drunk. Let your hair down. You have so much of it. Mother, here is some change. Make her do the laundry. Promise me that."

She was at her most treasured spot, deep within the cool recesses of her body. She laid down on its soft floor and stretched out to let its dark comfort gently settle over her.

Lights glittered at the entrance. The old voice was there. She smelled its sick.

"Rosie?"

She told legs to walk, and they carried her around the room while she asked arms, who were more finicky than legs and so had to be approached politely, to pick up clothes and put them into a pillow case. Generally, if properly addressed, arms did what they were asked, but hands, and especially fingers, dropped almost as much as they picked up. Naughty fingers. But they were good. They were good because they were body. Body was good because it was her. Not like talk. Talk was just words. When people talked, they lost body. They got thin. The more they talked the thinner they got, until one day they were really thin, really thin, like the figures in movies. She liked movies. Movies were just movies. Even the earthquake kind.

"Rosie? What are you doing? Leave the clothes. Don't go out. It's too late to go to that laundry. Leave them. I'll do them tomorrow. I'll feel better tomorrow. I'm sure I will. Rosie? It's too dangerous. Don't go baby."

The voice wanted to get close. It always wanted to do that. It wanted to get in and take her space. There was no room. There was only enough for her. It was her body.

"Hello."

"Oh, Rosie, Rosie."

At the Laundromat, the machines were quiet but not asleep.

They were expecting her, their lids open, ready to be fed. In the back, the flames of the refinery reflecting in their giant eyes, the dryers watched every move, even though they were to see what they had seen before, more than once.

He's here. In the corner. Watch him.

He's getting close. Why does he always want to get close. Make him talk so he won't be so close.

"Hello."

Talk. Why doesn't he talk. He never talks. Everyone else does. That's what people do. They talk. Make him say words so he will get thin.

"Hello."

If he said one word, any word, he'd be away. He wouldn't be here. Make him thin.

"Hello."

Why can't he stay away. It's my body. It belongs to me. He's breaking through. Don't cry. Whatever the hurt.

"Hello."

Fight him. Hit him. Hit him hard. But don't cry, don't cry, don't cry.

LOS DESCONOCIDOS

By star light, he crossed the patio to stand at its center. Early mornings fascinated him. They always had: as a kid, on the home place in East Texas; in the Marines, on Okinawa, even though the day brought fresh killing; and later, in college, when he wasn't nursing a hangover. His wife, who would sleep 'til noon if she had half a chance, discovered that was the first of an increasing number of his habits that irritated her.

Stars were so far away. They were there, each differing from the others, and the ones here in Mexico different again. They were so far away, and now in his widsom, they called to him.

Next to the stars, he liked the roosters. Mexico had plenty of roosters. They were crowing now; the ones he could hardly hear, by Insurgentes, the closer ones, by Puente de Alvarado, and finally, the one next door. In this short time, when the stars called, roosters owned the city.

He crossed the patio to piss around the banana plant. Of all the plants in the patio, the carnations in their pots, the gladiolas against the wall, the roses in front, he only pissed around the banana. It flourished, bearing fruit, which Julio, the gardener, claimed. Julio marveled at the smell surrounding the plant and how from such a stench sweet fruit could grow. "*¡Qué banano! ¡Qué fruta magnífica!*

He returned to his windowless room beneath the stairs that curved up from the patio to the galleries above. The room was scarcely big enough for his cot, but he had managed to squeeze in a stool that Doña Leonor had found for him. On the stool he placed the battered remnants of a hot plate, another gift from the Doña, and heated water for his coffee.

At sunup, Doña Leonor rang; he recrossed the patio to the giant doors with an equally impressive door key.

"*Buenos días,*" Doña Leonor greeted him, along with her daily accusation, "*Está flaco.*" Her concern over how thin he was, well intentioned from a mother of six, with the oldest nearly grown, threatened to snare him, but now, in his maturity, he had outgrown concern.

"Buenos días," he replied, and because she expected him to, he followed her as she began her day's work.

They started where she always did, with the director's office. She first swept, then dusted. At the huge desk, she held up the wedding picture of the director and his wife, he in formal gray, she in virginal white. Dona Leonor directed him to behold their happiness. *"Mire la pareja tan divina."* Careful to replace the picture in its exact location, so as not to disturb the marital ectasy, she confided in him with the certainty of knowledge gained third or fourth hand that the young señora already was *embarazada*; she glowed with pride over the director's prowess.

The desk finished, she dusted the gory crucifix next to the framed portrait of the head *político* of the Institutional Revolutionary Party, and with the water he brought, she mopped the already spotless floor clean again. Satisfied, she closed the office door gently, and with more dispatch turned to the lesser jobs of the day.

They were working up in the galleries when Julio rang. At the door, Julio grunted. He grunted in return. Julio was as small as Doña Leonor and as old, probably older, than he was. Thin, too, but skin brown, creased, and tough—as tough as the brown eyes that squinted under gray brows in deadly calculation.

Once, when he was drinking, and driven by the bottle's need, he had got Julio drunk. In response, Julio recounted how as a kid no older than five, he personally had welcomed Villa to the city. So impressed was Villa at Julio's enthusiasm, the generalissimo swooped him up to ride in front of him on Siete Leguas. People applauded, the horse pranced, and Julio waved. The memories and the tequila bringing tears, Julio concluded his drunk with all twelve verses of the corrido, "The Death of Pancho Villa."

He no longer had the need to get others drunk so they would talk to him, so he had stopped drinking and Julio had stopped talking. They grunted at each other. Julio got out his machete, his only gardening tool, and as he dug around the banana, he marveled, *"¡Qué banano! ¡Qué fruta magnifica!"* but what a terrible stench.

A few minutes before 10 A.M., opening time, the receptionist rang. Nails aglow, hair sealed in place, and heels clicking, she swept passed him, a polite *"Buenos días"* lingering in her perfume. At her desk, she got out her compact to touch a hand to hair and a Kleenex to incandescent lips. She asked for more pamphlets to distribute to the visitors and handed him the key to the metal cabinet by her chair.

At 10 A.M. he took down his uniform from its nail on the wall. When he bought it years ago at the Caballo Hierro, it was a snug fit over his 200 pounts. Now, it hung over his bones like a distant, second skin.

Dressed for his office, he swung open the heavy, wooden doors and latched them in place. Unless today was different, and that wasn't likely, few visitors would appear before 1 P.M.; and at 1, the museum closed until 4 P.M. From 4 until he shut the doors at 7 P.M., tourists on their way to the Bellas Artes, to the Cathedral, to Sanborns, would venture by. They paused in the doorway and took in the patio, the plants, and the receptionist. On seeing her and realizing this was something to visit, they checked their watches, consulted one another, and then, some at least, approached her. Behind her desk, she handed them the pamphlets, asked them to sign the attendance book, and collected the fee, all in one incandescent gush. Momentarily stunned, they opened the pamphlet, consulted again with one another, in crisp British, in quick Japanese, or, although less in these days of tales of drugs and corruption, in midwestern American, as to which gallery to see first. Decisions eventually arrived at, they climbed the stairs to wander among the oil portraits of the eighteenth and nineteenth century and to ponder the mythological scenes of the few seventeenth century paintings the museum possessed.

Officially, he was there to offer guided tours, available *"al público de 12:00 a 13:00 hrs."* But since few came at those hours, for the most part and for most days, he stood in the corners to insure no one's baby smeared candy or worse on the beard of an eighteenth century Spanish count.

Shortly before noon the director arrived. They all, Doña Leonor from the back, Julio from his plants, the receptionist from her desk, and he from the galleries, gathered to stand in review. The director paraded in front of them so they might admire his dark blue suit, his dazzling white shirt, his sparkling teeth, his moustache, penciled in, it would seem, above fleshy lips, and his thick, black hair, carefully coiffed over appreciative ears.

Basking in what he knew was freely bestowed approval, the director was their *patrón* and they, his *peones*. He toured the patio and instructed Julio as to the proper care of his plants. *"Oye muchacho,"* he, who was young enough and ignorant enough to be Julio's grandchild, *"Este banano huele horriblemente."* And Julio, who had ridden with Villa, was forced to consent that *"Si, señor director,"* the banana smelled bad, but that from such foul soil, the plant, with the help of God and the knowing hand of Julio, produced beautiful fruit, *una fruta suprema, sumamente suprema.*

Mollified, if not overcome by Julio's endorsement, the director

made for his office. "*Tráigame el café*," he called, and because even
he, *el señor director*, was addressing Doña Leonor, he ended his command with a respectful *por facor*.

Her very apron giving dignity to the task, Doña Leonor
crossed the patio with the coffee, but returned to say to him, "*El
director quiere verlo.*"

He knocked at the door and waited for the eventual ¡*Adelante*!
Inside, the director forced him to wait again while the director
finished his review of the day's correspondence; so he waited. The
last directive from the Instituto Nacional de las Artes Cultivadas
perused and with equal attention laid aside, the director looked at
him; so he looked back.

He stood somewhere between Julio, the "boy," and Leonor, the
Doña; consequently, the director did not know what to do with him;
consequently, the director disliked him. Disliked him so much, the
director would fire him, except the same official in the Instituto Nacional who appointed the director had also secured him his job.

In the days following World War II, he, with his GI Bill, and
the official, with his father's pesos, spent their nights with mariachi
and tequila and their days in the newly established American
School with aching heads. He took a little art, took a little archaeology, played a little football, got hurt and had to quit, got married
and got divorced, got drunk and got sober, most of the time, until
somewhere in the 1950s he woke up broke. The official, having
spent a year or so cultivating contacts with presumed important
personages at the American School, returned to a more conventional and more successful career in law. So when he found *himself*
out of money and out of luck, the official had found *himself* a comfort-
able place in the bureaucracy of cultivating the arts. The official
recalled fondly the days, or rather the nights, of their youth and
because of that fondness and perhaps also because he enjoyed the
prospect of dispensing favors to a downed gringo, the official offered
him the position of assistant director in charge of art at the museum—a position with possibilities, the official assured him. He
was grateful for the position but ignored the possibilities until,
while directors came and went, and went up, he stood before the
present one, a mixture of night watchman, guard, and guide; a mixture he didn't mind, but one the director disliked.

As if he could no longer stand the sight, the director shifted
his view from him to his nails. Comforted by their appearance, the
director announced that in the afternoon he personally would conduct a tour of the galleries for a group of important friends. With
that, the director dismissed him.

Since it was 1:00 P.M. he closed the doors in the face of an astonished couple who at that very moment had arrived. He crossed the patio to his room, ate the tortilla curled around rice and meat that Doña Leonor had pressed upon him, stretched out on his cot, and fell asleep. In his sleep, he dreamt of the first time he had heard the pictures talk. As was the actual occasion, it was a pleasant dream; he was reluctant to leave it when, close to 4:00 P.M. his eyes opened. He got up, eyed the banana plant, but contented himself with the toilet behind it.

Minutes before closing, the group arrived. By then both Doña Leonor and Julio had left, Doña with her ¡*Que flaco está Usted*! and Julio with his grunt. The receptionist longed to leave but dared not; she consulted her compact as if it would give her the answer. Once the group had strolled by her desk, she managed to get a whisper to the director, and in response to his curt nod, she vanished.

The group eventually made its way to the galleries. He walked behind with the facts the director would need should one of the group actually inquire about a date, a style, or a technique. In front, close to the director, a woman, blond, eyes shadowed, and sinuous in black, made appreciative swells with her jeweled bosom; the director responded with his voice rising high in excitement, descending low for solemnity, and pausing dramatically. When they passed what was reported to be Rubens' *Diana In Hunt*, he wondered if the woman recognized the sisterhood.

The painting always brought back his marriage. His wife, of course, was Diana, but he never figured out if he was the hound baying at her side or the stag with her spear rammed through its guts.

In the next gallery, the group discussed the subject of where they would dine later that evening. While they debated the pros and cons of Chinese over Lebanese, he positioned himself next to the only picture in the museum that didn't talk.

The portrait was a man in his maturity, seated next to a small table with one arm resting on the table and the other in his lap. He looked directly at the painter with soft gray eyes and with a gentle smile at play on his full lips. A man of substance, no doubt, with traces of nobility lingering in his nineteenth century composure.

"A damn Polack," he muttered in amazement, when he discovered the portrait in the back of the museum's storage room. What documents he unearthed attributed the painting to Ladislas de Czachorski, but as hard as he searched, in the museum's files and in the national archives, he could not discover who was the man Czachorski had painted.

"A damn Polack." On Okinawa, you could always tell it was a Polack who got hit because they bled more, and the bood richer and thicker, so that the stain on the sterile sand kept darker, longer.

When the museum was between directors, he had moved the portrait to its present corner. On the label to identify it, he had printed "Ladislas de Czachorski (1850–1911)," and the title *"Un hombre desconocido."*

The group, having reached a decision where to spend the evening, moved quickly through the remaining galleries, and by 8:00 P.M. he closed the doors behind them.

With the doors bolted, he returned to the galleries to listen to the pictures. He could not understand what they were saying, but it was talk. They commented to one another, asked each other questions, replied with brief affirmations, or at times, with more detailed explanations with reference to preceding points of discourse. The talk was pleasant and animated, but the pictures never argued or scolded one aother. When they, being courteous, addressed him for his opinion, he, even if he could not understand them, but wanting also to be polite, would nod his head in consent.

Sometimes he went from gallery to gallery to hear the changing tempo and tone of their talk, for each gallery had a different topic to consider, but for the most part he stood next to the Czachorski portrait, and the two shared their silence.

Tonight, as he stood by the portrait, he wanted to put out his hand, but that would be a queer thing to do, to hold hands with another man, particularly one in a picture. So he simply stayed next to the frame and listened.

Near midnight, the pictures stopped. He went downstairs to the banana plant to take a final piss and then to bed and sleep.

The cot moved. His eyes opened. The cot moved. The door to his room swung wide, and in the dark, the roosters crowed. The times before, when this had happened, he had been afraid. Now, in his late sixties, he was ready. Outside, the stars reeled across the sky; and their call rang in his ears.

He stumbled up the swaying stairs. Behind him, the steps crashed into his room below. The floors heaved, but he crossed the galleries to the portrait Czachorski had painted of a man unknown.

A shudder threw him to his knees, and with a screech, the adjacent gallery collapsed. Diana would hunt no more. He got to his feet and was hurled against the portrait. He looked into the soft gray eyes and kissed the smile on the full lips. "Damn Polack."

He unhooked the portrait from the wall, wrapped his arms around it, and stood there, ready.

It was more than a week before the bulldozers reached the museum, but when the driver ran his blade across the body, he backed off and got his chief to call the disposal squad.

"*¿Quién es?*" Who is it, he asked the two men with hankerchiefs tied around their faces and the body between them. "*¿Quién sabe?*" Who knows, came the reply. "*Otro hombre desconocido.*"

CRY LONESOME

A NOVELLA

PROLOGUE

The narrator of this episodic novella and the narrator of this prologue share several passions. They both believe that since January 1, 1953, country music has gone steadily downhill, that Miguel de Unamuno wrestled with God in a contest that ended in at least a draw, and that anthropology speaks, as does no other scholarly endeavor, to the magnificence of being human. Certain differences, however, need to be noted. The narrator of the novella is a World War II vet, while the narrator of the prologue is a veteran of the Korean Conflict; the novella's narrator's wife is much younger than he, the wife of the prologue's narrator is closer to his age and much nicer; and, the most important difference of all, the narrator of the prologue has a name.

I

THE WOODS BURNER

When I first heard of the fire, it was a morning like today: a crisp, cool, mid-October morning, the kind that always makes me glad, after all these years, that I live in Louisiana. I was up early that morning, a year ago, grateful to get away from Joanna. Don Miguel was surprised but quite pleased to have his Cat Chow. I had the radio on WKSL in the faint hope that I would hear a real country tune, when the 5:00 A.M. news announced:

> Sheriff James Wright reported a late night fire north of Mt. Hope on a tract owned by the New Jersey and Atlantic. The fire, now under control, destroyed approximately twenty-five acres of timber and, from the last accounts, the residence of well-known lobbyist, Jules Delacroix. The house, not presently occupied, was a total loss. The cause of the fire remains under investigation.
>
> Stay tuned to WKSL, the station that brings you the latest in news and the best in country music. Here is Barbara Mandrell and one of her biggest hits, 'I Was Country When Country Wasn't Cool.'

"And babe, I was country before you were born," I told Barbara in disgust and carried my cereal to the back porch. Miguel came to waited impatiently for me to finish so he could lick the bowl. He had appeared on the front steps about a year ago—shortly after Joanna's father had carried her "home," the general said, "to Dallas"—and announced his arrival in loud and, what I took to be, declarative statements. He was a white cat with brown markings on his body and two dark spectacles around studious eyes. Given the learned nature of his appearance and, considering the no-nonsense character of his voice, I named him after the philosopher, novelist, poet, and self-styled "alarm clock of sleeping souls," Miguel de Unamuno, which was quickly shortened to Don Miguel, and then, sometimes to Miguel, but never to the diminutive Miguelito.

I watched Don Miguel finish the bowl and leap upon Joanna's chaise longue to improve an already superior countenance. October was a good month for burning. The pine straw piled up from last year was dry and the wind not too strong.

For the last hundred years and more, the small landowner in Fredonia Parish had raised crops, cattle, and hogs, and more important to his existence, hunted small game and run deer with dogs. In a cycle of care that went back to the Choctaw—and not a few claimed Indian blood, even if always "on my mamma's side"—the farmer cleaned his land each fall with fire. The fire cleared out the underbrush, kept the ticks under control, and improved the pasture for both cattle and deer. A cleansed forest in the fall made the land ready, in a moral sense, for spring's new birth.

The big paper and lumber companies, like the NJ&A had a different view. In their accounting, fire was an expense and the woods burner a threat to profits. So they declared war. Signs sprouted from fence posts along the roadside to warn of prosecution, fines, and prison. On television, Smokey the Bear spoke, in somber, Walter Cronkite tones, of how "Forest fires hurt everyone," and in the background a tearful fawn picked her way through the scourged landscape in vain search for her lost mother. Rural sociologists, their tenure secured with company grants, sent graduate students to assault harried housewives with "Please answer the following, yes or no. 'Forest fires are detrimental to the economic well-being of our community.'"

The signs, the bear, and the sociologists won the war. They turned the woods burner from a shepherd of the forest into a wild-eyed, pinched-face pyromaniac with a neurotic grudge against progress, and profits.

The war was won about the time the USDA Forest Service decided that controlled burning promoted both deer and pine. By then it was too late. Victorious in war, the companies lost the peace, and woods burning turned ugly. When the NJ&A began weeding the hardwoods from a tract in the northern part of the parish—wood that fed small game and feral hogs—nervous company ax-men heard the whistle of bullets. The next day, even more nervous, they found cardboard signs spray painted red: "You ring the oaks? We'll burn the pines."

"What do you think, Don Miguel? *¿Cómo le parece a Usted?*" I asked in two languages. But *el gran agonista*, from his position in the exact center of Joanna's chair and with his head now at rest upon his outstretched paws, refused to comment. I gave him a stroke on the head, which he accepted as his just due, and went back to the kitchen.

The radio had called it the "residence of well-known lobbyist,

Jules Delacroix." Jules was well-known all right, too well-known for some. Even his friends wondered if his relationship with certain state officials, and their secretaries, wasn't overly cozy. Only the media, however, called the house his residence. Everyone else called it what it had been since the Civil War, the "Howard place." The Howards were also well-known, and as powerful, and about as popular, as the NJ&A. Could be that someone, with a little liquor in him, decided to even the score. October was a good month for burning.

I added the cereal bowl to the dirty stack in the sink and went into the bedroom where each night Joanna came to fill my sleep with guilt. What if I cleaned out her closet? But what would I do with her clothes? Her shoes? Her purses? I even had the dress, a blue silk, she insisted on wearing when I took her to the hospital. "If I am going there to die, I want to look my best."

I couldn't give them away. They belonged to Joanna. What if I burned them? What if I made a pile of the clothes, the shoes, the purses, the blue silk, poured on the guilt, and then struck a match? Could I then sleep? Sleep a sleep without guilt? Sleep the sleep of the dead?

I pressed the on-switch, and the voice in the bedside clock radio explained:

The New Orleans Saints, searching for a successful combination, traded their first round draft choice for veteran quarterback, Joe Rigoletto, and a player to be named later.

Back home, before WW II, a lot of people didn't have radios. Not just colored people either. The first one my daddy brought home was a monster. Taller than me. Now there was one in nearly every room.

Rigoletto, once famous for the long bomb, said his experience under fire would help stabilize the up-and-down Saints.

But the only TV we had was a small black and white we turned on for the news. Joanna disliked TV almost as much as she disliked country music. When we first met, I tried to explain about Hank, and what he meant to people like me. She even made herself listen to a song or two, "Howlin' at the Moon," and "I Just Told Mamma Goodbye." But she let me know she preferred Joan Baez. Funny, people who said back in the 60s they found folk music refreshing didn't like Hank. Now, here in the 1980s, you didn't hear Joan or Hank.

Locally, the Foresters have a week off to prepare for their annual homecoming game with the Cajuns from bayou land. The Foresters have had their own problems, but a win over their arch rivals would make their season and guarantee, some say, Coach Hunnicutt another year at the helm.

I put on whatever clothes I had handy, got my briefcase, checked the cat door was open, and went out the front door. In the overgrown yard, I picked the *Messenger* out of the weeds. Down at the bottom of the front page was a notice that Dr. Forrest Hollingsworth, former president of the University of South Louisiana, had been admitted to the Mt. Hope Confederate Memorial for observation. But the *Messenger* must have gone to press before the fire. I tossed the paper and briefcase into the seat of my 1965 Chevrolet pickup, and after some choking, got it started. I sputtered my way through Reed's Town, and at Edelstein's Jewelry turned left on to Main. To the north, smoke from the NJ&A stacks rose straight as an arrow in the clear, pure October air.

II

WILD BILL

The sign said Lawrence G. Wilson, which wasn't my name but I fumbled for a key stamped 43 and let myself in. The day I retired, two years ago, the University informed me that, in light of my years of service, they in turn would allow me to share a broom closet in the basement of Freiburgh Hall. So I moved from my office—the one I had used ever since Joanna and I returned in 1964 from dissertation fieldwork in Mexico—into Wee Willie's. Actually, as big as he was, Wee Willie didn't take up much space, simply because he was around so little. He made it in on Monday, Wednesday, and Friday, taught his four sections of "Marriage and the Family," and by 1:30 P.M., he was gone. So I practically had the place to myself.

I took the coffee pot to the men's room, dumped out the grounds, filled it, and came back. The coffee perking, I unpacked my briefcase. Even before the sickness, Joanna had complained about how hard I worked, "You're trying to get a heart attack, aren't you. Don't expect me to sit around, holding your hand, mopping your brow." Before the sickness spread through her, I worked hard, and now, harder.

I poured the coffee and, waiting for my thoughts to start, I cleaned my nails with the blade of my Ka-Bar. Back home, when a boy started shaving, he got a Marlin 22 rifle and a Ka-Bar pocket knife, with a three-inch blade. The Depression and hard times came with my first whiskers, so I was lucky to get a Daisy air gun and a Woolworth, tin-blade special. The first thing I bought when I sold the pigs from a sow my older brother gave me was the Ka-Bar I now had in my hand.

Thoughts of the past, loose and worn, clattered through my head, but thoughts of the future, tight and new, would hardly turn

over. So, nails cleaned and trimmed down to the nub, I poured a second cup.

The bookcase beside my desk was nearly full. Two shelves contained library volumes, but the rest held my favorites, Unamuno, of course, but also Ernest Becker and Loren Eiseley. There was a biography of Hank next to the first book I had bought, when, fresh from Okinawa and lucky to be alive, I enrolled in college: *Webster's New Collegiate Dictionary.* "Look at the words," I remembered running my finger up and down the pages. "I've got to know them. I've got to know them all."

On the bottom shelf, collecting dust, sat a three volume Modern Library edition of Gibbon's *Decline and Fall of the Roman Empire.* My English teacher at East Texas had pronounced that no man might call himself educated until he had read Gibbon. I struggled through the first half of the first volume, but despite almost nightly promises, I had never gotten further; nor had, I now suspect, the English professor.

Warmed by the coffee, my thoughts were starting up, when Wee Willie blustered in, five minutes before his 7:30 section.

"You hear about the fire?"

"The Howards?"

"They say it was a woods fire that got loose. If I'da known that woulda happen, I'da set it myself."

Wee Willie's father was one of the tenant farmers Matthew Howard had kicked off during the middle of the Depression when he had abandoned both cotton and people and turned his land into trees.

"Them Howards finally gettin' what they deserve. A Cajun son-in-law spendin' up all their money. A daughter whorin' around. And now somebody decides the woods ought to burn. If that little wood fire happens to take their house, you don't see no tears in my eyes."

Willie's spite made me uneasy, so I asked, "Who do the Rebs play this Saturday?"

"Vandy," he answered with a sneer.

"Vanderbilt is not bad. Last week, they held State to three TDs and scored twice themselves."

"State," Willie replied, sneer upon sneer. "A bunch of bell ringin' goat ropers." And with that summation, Willie left for class, not a note in his hand.

In high school, Willie had lettered four years at tackle. His senior year, he weighed 230, and the Tigers wanted him badly, but Willie's folks were from Mississippi, so he crossed the Pearl to sign with Johnny Vaught up in Oxford. Willie was star bound, but the night of Billy Cannon's run, a downfield block wrecked his knee. He managed to get his bachelor's in phys ed and hung on until they gave him a M. Ed. in social studies.

His desk was empty except for a half-finished pack of Beechnut, the current copy of *Penthouse,* and an out-of-date textbook titled, with unconscious irony, *Marriage in the Modern Era.* I wondered what Willie taught. Maybe he drew on experience. He had been married longer than his students had lived, and despite his tendency to wander afield, Helen and he would stay that way. Like Willie, Helen was a local Mt. Hope girl, and when she was growing up, anyone with a high school diploma was a fine catch. Willie's possession of a master's degree made him truly remarkable, almost as remarkable as his football exploits. So Helen considered herself fortunate. Unlike, I could not keep myself from saying, Joanna.

"Why can't we leave here?" Every fall, the academic spring, the time for renewed dedication, Joanna asked her questions. "Why can't we go to North Carolina? To Oregon? Why must we stay here?"

A figure stood at the door. W. Charles Elliot. He entered my life two years ago, and at times, I wondered what I did for aggravation before he came.

"Come in, Charles. Have some coffee?"

"No thank you. May I ask your reaction to the news?"

"About the fire?"

"What fire?"

"The Howard place."

"The Howard place?"

"The big house of a big family north of town. It burned early this morning. Lucky, no one was home. A woods fire broke loose."

"It was intentional?"

"Could be. The Howards are good at collecting enemies."

"As a native participant, but as an anthropological observer, do you consider this incident an example of the syndrome referred to as the South's penchant for violence?"

Unable to respond, I groped for the coffee and poured more on my desk than in my cup.

"Do you?"

I now understood how natives felt about their anthropologists. Being the object of someone's dispassionate curiosity, however well considered, lacked a lot. I could almost see W. Charles taking notes.

"Perhaps," I reluctantly agreed.

When he finished his mental recordings, W. Charles said, "I was referring to the President's announcement."

Now it was my turn, "What announcement?"

"I had forgotten you were retired. President Coleman has launched a campaign to change the name of our University."

Our University? Thirty years and more I've been here. Gordon Coleman took Intro to Anthro from me, and barely made a *B*. And you? Where were you, W. Charles Elliot? No more than a gleam in your daddy's eyes?

"The President proposed to change the name from the University of South Louisiana to the University of Louisiana."

Sounding more like a press release than a young man barely twenty five with a dissertation still pending, W. Charles made it clear that "the change of the name simply encapsulates all the changes—modern new buildings, increased library acquisitions, and addition of new faculty—that have moved the University from being a regional school concerned almost exclusively with teaching to being an institution of national, if not international, import.

Charles went on at length about how "we" had gotten so much better, especially during the last two years, and particularly with, he quoted again, "the infusion of fresh talent recruited from the major universities across the nation, including," here Charles spoke in italics, "*Cornell*."

"The President specifically mentioned the development of doctoral programs and implied that anthropology is slated for additional enhancement. If so, I am confident we will shortly offer the doctorate."

Elliot's enthusiasm amused me. During the boom days of the '60s, when salaries were doubling and grants were for the asking, the only intellectuals who came to the region came for a quick fix for their conscience and dashed back to brag how they had been with King at Selma. Now, with the recession, they were flocking south like ducks. Strangely, this time they said little about Selma and not a word about King.

Even so, listening to Charles, hearing him make plans, and watching the eagerness grow in his eyes, I felt the old desire to build, to put together, to construct how the future might come to be. Having for years been the lone anthropologist at the University, and, when I first came, the only one in the state, teaching every subject from biological evolution to language and culture—expounding in one class on the significance of bipedality in the australopithecines and the very next hour arguing the Sapir-Whorf hypothesis of linguistic determinism—and realizing with every breath how inadequate I must sound and how poorly prepared I was to carry forth the cause of my discipline, I rejoiced that new faces, each with a specialty, each with new knowledge, had appeared. I longed to tell Charles the pride I had in his arrival. But he wouldn't shut up. And here was Willie.

"Class over?"

"I let 'em out early."

Charles raised his eyebrows and breathed a disdainful Cornell "Oh?" Willie picked up the Beechnut, packed a wad in his mouth, and leaned back in his chair; his enormous jaws chomped on the tobacco. He kicked a wastebasket into the middle of the room, arched a dark blob at it, and wiping his mouth on a sleeve, repeated, his eyes fixed on Charles, "I said, goddamn it, I let 'em out early."

W. Charles Elliot and Wee Willie Wilson: The one a young, lean, Ivy Leaguer, who read Wittgenstein in the original gothic; the other an old, fat, Bush League Player, who never picked up anything heavier than the *Sporting News*.

W. Charles, his face transfigured into incredulous condescension, looked to me, a fellow professional and a Ph.D. like he soon would be, but I would have none of it. Instead, I asked,

"W. Charles Elliot, what does the W. stand for?"

"William, why?"

Willie, quick in his own way, jumped right on it. "William Elliot?"

"Yes, of course."

Willie pretended to tilt a hat back on his head, stuck his thumbs in his belt, and walked bowlegged over to W. Charles. He made several exaggerated chews on the Beechnut, spit again in the basket, stuck his face in front of Charles, and drawled, "Wild Bill, this town ain't big enough for the both of us."

"What is this all about?" W. Charles asked.

"Never mind," I said, laughing at Willie's gunfighter. "Watch out, Willie. They say he's peaceful, but don't get him riled."

"Come on. Tell me, you guys. What's the joke?"

"Oh, it's nothing."

"If it is nothing, then I am leaving."

Willie blocked his way. "Wild Bill, you fast as they say?"

Charles tried to go around, but Willie wouldn't let him.

"Draw," he commanded.

"What?" W. Charles managed a weak laugh. He tried a step toward the door, but stopped again by Willie's fleshy bulk, he pulled back, his face red. "All right, when you have had your fun, tell me."

Willie stalked after him, "Draw."

Charles pushed a chair at Willie, and before Willie could brush it aside, he dashed for the door, tripping, almost falling, over the

wastebasket. At the door, he turned to me, this time with hurt in his voice, "Upgrading this place is going to be a real challenge."

The Ph.D. in me made me want to follow Charles and to apologize, but my League, like Wee Willie's, played here in the South, and to Willie, after W. Charles had left, I asked, "I wondered if you would remember?"

"Oh sure. Wild Bill Elliot. Wore his guns butt forward and had a paint horse. Sometimes, he'd have a sidekick, Gabby Hayes, maybe, or Fuzzy Knight, one of them funny guys."

"Cannonball?"

"Who? Cannonball? Sure it was. Cannonball Taylor. Head as bald as a baby's butt. Sure it was, but more of the time, you know, Wild Bill, he rode alone, him and that paint. A real gentleman. Tipped his hat to the ladies and said, 'yes 'um,' but not a sissy like Gene Autry. No sir. Some fancy gambler or a crooked banker, and hell they all crooked as a dog's leg, one of them might waltz up to Wild Bill with the idea they'd push him around. 'How did you come by that name?' they'd say. Wild Bill now, he look at 'em with them steel gray eyes of his, hook his thumbs in his belt, lean back on his heels a bit, and say just loud enough they had to strain to hear, 'They call me Wild Bill, but I'm a peaceful man.' "

"Next to Johnny Mack Brown, he was my favorite. You understand Johnny Mack played football, and I always sided with him, even if he did play for Alabama.

"Every Saturday, me and my cousin spend the whole afternoon in the Ritz for a dime. It was only a block from the house. That's after them Howards screwed us royal, and we had to move to town. Times was hard. All my daddy knew was plowin' an' hoein'."

"The same with mine."

"I didn't know you was a farm boy."

"Raised on one."

"That the truth? Plowin' an' hoein' was all my daddy had. That and us kids. But he'd find a dime for Saturdays. And we did enjoy that dime. At the Ritz, they'd have serials."

"Flash Gordon?"

"Buster Crabbe did him. Buster Crabbe, now he was handsome, good-looking man. An athlete, too. A swimmer. Was in the Olympics, too. I forget. In the '30s."

"1932."

"Yeah, 1932? Maybe. You know how Wild Bill got his name? Played Wild Bill Hickok in a serial, and from then on, naturally, he was Wild Bill."

"Back home, people liked Tex Ritter."

"I'd imagine, being a Texan. I wasn't much on them singers myself, but I did like old Bob Nolan in the Sons of the Pioneers."

"Better than Roy Rogers."

"Oh yeah."

"Willie, did you know he wasn't much over sixty the day he died?"

"Who?"

"Wild Bill."

"No shit."

"Willie?"

"What?"

"Tex Ritter, Bob Nolan, Buster Crabbe, Wild Bill, they're all gone. Willie?"

"What, goddamn it."

"Willie, who's going next? Willie?"

III

IN MEMORIAM

"Doc," the voice said on the phone. "We found a body."

Uh-Oh, somebody got caught. Outside, the sheriff's Ford pulled up. I got in, Jimmy Junior nodded, and we were off.

Ordinarily, it took an hour to get from the University through town to the Howard place. Jimmy Junior made it in half that time. And, he might have said two words. Jimmy got it from his father, and his father from his. The Wrights—if that is who they were—disliked talking. Speaking was like screwing; it wasted a man.

The inarticulate South. The South that Faulkner, a Southerner, wrote about. The South that when it spoke, spoke in tongues. The South I was born into.

Silent, but not quiet, and not slow. Siren wailing, tires squealing, we roared down Main, crossed the Illinois Central with only the Ford's paint job between us and a New Orleans-bound diesel, scattered chickens and kids in the NJ&A Quarters, and once across the Tangipahoa and onto Highway 51, we were practically airborne. With the idea he wasn't above driving this way just to scare an old man and a university professor to boot, I stole a look at Jimmy. He seemed more absorbed with whatever was going on inside him than with his driving, and that made me even more nervous. Fortunately, we topped a rise, and there was the Howard place, or what the fire had left of it.

To the south of the house and to the north, bulldozers had knocked down strips of pines to contain the fire; in back, Jordan's Creek had prevented it from going east, and here in front, the highway had stopped it.

"Don't know yet," Jimmy Junior had managed to get his mouth working, "if the fire started at the house and spread, or if it started in the trees and took the house."

Like the family, the house had been a landmark. Built by Old Man Howard when the family's finances took an upswing after Reconstruction, the house was not the antebellum, white columned Scarlett O'Hara mansions up in Natchez, but it was, for the region, a large, attractive, two-story structure with a central hallway and chimneys at either end. Joanna had loved it. When DeeDee Howard and Jules Delacroix were married, Joanna and I, along with half of Fredonia Parish, were invited to the reception.

As I followed Jimmy from the car through the gate and across the yard to where his father stood at what had been the entrance,

Joanna pulled me through the crowd in the central hall and up the staircase. At the top, she turned us so that we looked down at the bright, well-dressed faces below, and she whispered fiercely, "Now this is what *I* was born to."

"The fire didn't leave much. Not of the house. Not of him," Sheriff Wright said, shaking my hand. "You know these two?" he waved toward the men nearby. I nodded and shook hands with Chief Otzenberger, from the Mt. Hope Fire Department, and with Oscar Davis, claims adjuster from Percy-Davis Insurance. Otzenberger already had his handkerchief out and was patting his face. In any weather, cold or hot, the chief sweated great oily drops that smelled of the home brew he made. Oscar, self-assured in sports coat and creased pants, with his freshly cut, yellow blond hair slicked back, hooted at the chief's discomfort. Both, the Chief in his sweat and Oscar in his assurance, were present because it was the Howard place that had burned.

"Well, let's look." The sheriff led us through the thick, gray layer of ashes and around the dark, unrecognizable mounds that only yesterday staged a family's life: huge tables where the old and the young, the wise and the foolish, the newly married and the recently divorced gathered to celebrate their kin, real and fictitious, with pork, beef, and turkey sliced thick with sterling silver and piled high on delicate china; full length mirrors where the ladies paused to admire a new dress from Maison Blanche's and to exclaim how handsome a visiting cousin had grown; and giant beds where the women slept, made love to their men, and, occasionally, and for good reasons, no doubt, wept.

The far end of the house was gone. Even the chimney had fallen. At this end, a few charred joists supported fragments of flooring; and the chimney rose mostly intact.

"And here's the nigger that did it," Oscar, ever ready to accuse, pronounced. I knelt at what my nose more than my eyes told me was a body. Burned human, I learned from Okinawa, where I had smelled both white and yellow, and far too many of either, stank no different from other charred flesh, but I always felt it should. Sweeter, maybe—or more bitter. I fumbled for the tools I didn't have and finally used my Ka-Bar to flick away the ashes. The fire had destroyed the extremities, and only the legs, the torso, and a portion of the upper arms remained.

"It's human, ain't it, Doc?" Jimmy Junior asked.

I had to smile to myself. Ever since Jimmy brought me a "hand" that turned out to be an alligator foot, he had been careful with his conclusions.

Oscar, who was not, demanded, "Where's that nigger's head?"

"In a hot fire like this one," Chief Otzenberger explained, "the skull blows up, doesn't it, Doc? I've heard 'em go. They sound like a twelve gauge. Boom."

"What do you think?" Sheriff Wright interrupted the chief's sound effects.

"It's human, all right," was all I could say. "Anyone missing?"

"When I called Mr. Delacroix this morning in Baton Rouge, he said as far as he knew the house was empty. He's worried, though. Several of the Howards have keys, and he says they often let themselves in to spend the night. He was to check with his wife." The sheriff paused and, reproach in his voice, added, "DeeDee is in Las Vegas."

"An old house like this," the chief kicked a joist for emphasis, "is built to burn. Anything might set it off. The wiring could. But if the woods caught first, the heat itself might ignite it. It'll be hell to figure out." The thought stimulated even more sweat, and the chief mopped away, his handkerchief now a sponge.

Oscar, as cool as when he sat behind his desk at his uncle's company or when he escorted people to their seats at the First Baptist where he already was a deacon, announced in his investigator's voice, "Before I can move on this claim, I am going to need a statement from you, Chief."

"You need shit, Oscar." Sweaty or not, the Chief wasn't going to be played with. "I'm only here because Sheriff asked me. And for all these years that I've been a friend to the Howards." And he added, just so Oscar would remember, "Friends long before you were born."

"What you want to do, Doc?" The sheriff ignored the exchange.

"I'll need a place to look him over." I had already decided, and without reason, the body was a man and, black or white, was old— old, alone, and at the edge of his life.

"The coroner won't want it."

"I can probably find a place at the University. We need a bag." Considering what little was left, I added, "and something to pick him up in."

"Jimmy Junior," the Chief called to Jimmy, who was already on his way to get a plastic bag from the Ford, "There's a shovel in my truck."

Jimmy knelt to hold open the bag, and I, also on my knees, eased in the pieces. Finished, I stayed down, and Jimmy stayed with me. Jimmy, who, when he spoke, spoke in tongues, looked at me, and I, I spoke not at all. But the only farewell the poor bastard was going to get was now and from us. Jimmy, wiser than I had ever

thought, offered his silence, and we, Jimmy Junior and I, Southerners, came together speechless before death.

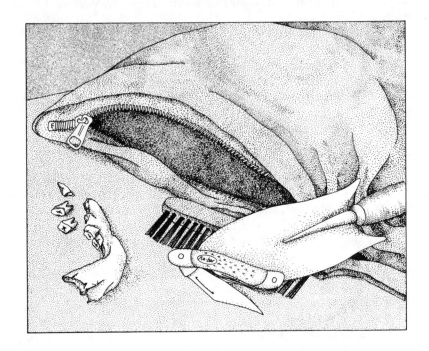

IV

FREEJACK FREEDOM

On the way back to town, Jimmy Junior drove slower, not
much, but enough so I could think ahead. Martha would not be
pleased if I showed up with a body. I had used her lab for my forensic cases before but that was when the lab was only an unused
weight room in the old gym. Now it was The Institute for Archaeological Research.

I escorted Martha Nijinska through the gym the year she
interviewed for the newly established archaeological position. The
year we learned about the tumor. The doctor had scarcely finished,
when Joanna pleaded, the first of many times, "Don't let me die in
Mt. Hope."

Martha's interview was in the spring of that year. The space
wasn't much to look at, a leftover weight machine, a pair of rings
dangling from the ceiling, and a long table, fortunately free of
forensic matters.

"It'll do," Martha interrupted my apologetic description. "For now."

The week Martha moved from Penn State she got rid of the weight machine, took down the rings, but kept the table. When Physical Plant was slow in their refurbishing, she spoke on the phone to the director. The next day the carpenters came early to install the shelving, and the day after, the painters arrived, brushes at the ready. Her first year Martha reexcavated a site dug by the WPA back in the '30s. To everyone's astonishment, her excavation established the presence of pre-pottery agriculture. Her second year, she published the discovery in a forceful account the reviewers called "daring but convincing." Now only in her third year, she was up for tenure, and Penn State wanted her back.

"Do you think Mr. Davis was right?" Jimmy Junior broke the silence we had shared.

"What?"

"When Mr. Davis said it," Jimmy nodded his head back at the body in the trunk, "was a nigger, was he right?"

When *Mr.* Davis, who was no more than a year older than Jimmy, said *nigger*, he said it with the nastiness you learn to expect from Oscar.

"Race is the hardest feature to determine about a body. Male, female, young, old, that's easy. A person is a man or a woman, a kid or an adult, and he dies? That's what he stays. But race? Race seems to disappear."

"A man's a nigger or not, ain't he?"

"That's what Oscar Davis would say, but the certainty is not the same."

"What you mean?"

More than simple curiosity was at work on Jimmy Junior. The Wrights, they said, were kin to the Reboues. The Reboues, along with the Syvads and the Melangons, lived south of Mt. Hope, on the last high ground before the land disappeared into the swamps around Lake Ponchartrain. The Reboues fished, hunted, and made their own liquor. They fired the swamp grass for their few head of brindle cattle and weren't all that concerned if the fire spread to the higher land and the better farms to the north. Neither black nor white was welcome, and their only visitors were bootleggers and people running from their past, a man from a too successful knife fight, or a woman from a too brutal husband.

The people in Mt. Hope called them "Freejacks," but not to their face. A local historian, noted for his ability for making the simple complicated, came up with a theory to explain both the name and the peculiar people attached to it. They were, he pronounced, the descendants of slaves freed by Andrew Jackson for their ferocious attacks against the Redcoats in the Battle of New Orleans. "Jackson freed 'em; so they're freed-jacks." The blacks in the NJ&A Quarters, themselves dark offsprings of field hands brought directly from West Africa, said in reply, that Freejacks weren't nothing but turpentine niggers, who in the past had made a living tapping trees and who had picked up a little brightening along the way.

The day after Pearl Harbor, Freejack men stood in line to sign up for the duration. The few who came back came with pale-skin wives they had acquired in the North or overseas in England. Before the Klan knew it, they had ex-Freejacks for neighbors. The Grand Wizard called a rally, but the next day they found the Grand Wizard in a ditch outside of town, his tongue sticking out his throat.

The former Freejacks became model citizens, which, in Mt. Hope, meant they joined the First Baptist and voted Democrat. Their children went to white schools, dated cheerleaders, and lived in ignorance of kinky-haired cousins. To purify their blood from any lingering stains, some changed their names, and nearly all became Mt. Hope's most vocal proponents of white supremacy.

Try though they might, they could not escape the memory of their origins, and the whispers that kept the memory alive and vicious. "They tell me Davis is just another way to spell Syvad," and "Scratch a Wright and it'll bleed Reboue."

"It seems to me," Jimmy Junior wouldn't let it go, "Mr. Davis is right. A nigger is a nigger."

"How do you bleed a Reboue?" I couldn't resist asking Mr. James *Wright*, Jr.

Jimmy flinched, but his pride, to its credit, kept him silent and his bleeding to himself.

Having paid Jimmy back for the wild ride, I said more professionally, "Race, in our society, is mainly a matter of the skin. Take away the skin, and you take away race. That's what the fire did. Were he alive, the man we found at the Howard place, people would know in an instant what he was. But the fire burned away his skin, and when it did, it burned away their certainty."

"Mr. Davis was awful certain."

"Davis? Certain? Tell me, Jimmy, how do you spell Syvad?"

Jimmy laughed. "Doc, for an outsider, you know a lot about us. Maybe," Jimmy slowed for a light at the edge of town. "Maybe you know too much."

An outsider? Who knew too much? Who knew more than he should? More than he had a right to know? Joanna would agree.

The Joanna of Mt. Hope. The Joanna of battles lost, of opportunities missed, of successes that spelled defeat.

"My life is an error," she concluded the night I told her I had been elected President of the Southern Anthropological Conference. "One Enormous Error. Professor Newberry, the foremost authority on Alexander Pope, told me that day I dropped his course to go to Mexico with you, I was his most brilliant student. He had made arrangements for me to spend a year in Oxford. Can you imagine," she consulted the ice in her third Scotch, "I chose Nueva Esperanza, Mexico, population 1,000, counting scorpions and rattlesnakes, over Oxford, England. 'His most brilliant student,'" she repeated the words to taste them once more before they turned sour and had to be washed away with the Scotch.

But that was the Joanna of Mt. Hope. Not the Joanna of New Orleans, of Sophie Newcomb, she a senior and I a graduate student; of Tulane, she in literature and I in anthropology; the Joanna of trust that bred desire.

"I want to know," I fumbled for a way to tell her the secret and explain its passion. "You want to know what?" she asked. We sat next to one another on a bench in Audubon Park among the Sunday strollers. Her hair was a gentle red, her face a soft white, and her eyes the bluest I ever fell into.

"All there is."

She laughed and laid her cool hand on my arm. "I love you."

The Joanna of Mt. Hope, of hope lost, who wrapped her bitterness in royal purple and proclaimed the reign of Joanna, The Mistake. "Perhaps if I had had children. But you were my child, my man child, my daddy boy. You grew up, and I was alone."

Finally, Joanna of the tumor. I in my middle sixties and pushed into retirement; she barely in her late forties and pushed into nothing. The tumor burned away her envy and, the months before the hospital, she resigned from her reign, cast aside the purple armor, and opened her arms so that I might once more lay my head between her breasts.

"Where to?" Jimmy Junior startled me. We were at the University gates.

The sign, The Institute for Archaeological Research, bright in my head, I replied, "The old gym."

I still had my key, and Jimmy helped me carry the body, encased in its green plastic shroud, inside to lay it, as in the past with other cases, including Jimmy's alligator "hand," on the large table. I walked back to the door with Jimmy, and he climbed into the sheriff's Ford.

"Doc," he called through the driver's window. I stepped down to the car. The moment we shared at the Howards' reappeared. "I just want to shake your hand."

With the Reboue bleeding checked, and his silence restored, Jimmy Junior, with tires squealing and siren wailing, was gone.

Inside, I rummaged through the drawers and lockers. Martha's archaeology did not include life, even dead life. To her, a potsherd, a spear point, or an arrowhead was more important than a femur, a pelvis, or even a skull. I found brushes, trowels, and shovels, but nothing resembling a dissecting kit. That didn't matter. Making-do was what I was good at. If ever I had all that I needed—all the equipment, bright, polished, and specialized, and all the assistants, trained, eager, and anticipating my instructions—I would have been stopped cold.

So I took a trowel and a brush, but after considering the shovels for a hard minute, I couldn't figure a use for them, so I moved on. In a file drawer with the keys in the lock, I found a camera and a roll of Kolorchrome ASA 64, a little slow but with all the lights on, it might do.

I unzipped the bag and pulled the edges of the dark plastic back away from the body. I loaded and focused the camera, but the indicator read on the low side. I got a roll of paper towels from the supply on the bottom shelf of a glass cabinet, and with the trowel I raised up the edges of the corpse and tucked the paper underneath. I focused the camera. Still too low. I unscrewed Martha's desk lamp, clamped it to the table, and ran an extension from the plug behind the desk to the table. I focused again. Just right. I was halfway through the roll, when Martha came in.

"I thought you had retired," her annoyance ill-concealed. Noticing the camera and with sarcasm dripping, she added. "Find everything you need?" By then she was close enough to see what I was photographing. She went through various colors of the rainbow and then settled on green. "What's that?" her sarcasm swept away by the breakfast she was trying to keep down.

Martha's question made me lower the camera and instead of a corpse on a table, I saw him, the one who had no reason for being in the Howard mansion, unless he were the fire-starter. Once started, the fire searched for its maker, found him, embraced him, and in its greed, consumed the house itself. Its food devoured, the fire, exhausted and now dying, curled around its creator for a final caress.

What was left lay on my table: no legs, no arms, not even a head, the brain boiling with the heat until the skull exploded, shattering it and leaving only jaw fragments and teeth. But the teeth spoke. Worn smooth, broken and missing, they whispered his life. I leaned forward to nod in understanding.

"What is it?" Martha came close as if afraid.

"A man," I replied.

"Where is he from?"

I looked at the teeth, but Martha's question had hushed them. Later, when I was alone, perhaps they would speak again.

"I don't know."

"Where did you find him?"

"The Howard place," and I told her of Jimmy Junior's call, the silent, wild hurtle through town, through the NJ&A Quarters, across the Tangipahoa, north on Highway 51, to the house, where, circled by burned pine, stood a single, naked chimney, separated from its collapsed twin by the dark ruin through which walked Sheriff Wright, worried the body might, after all, be a Howard; claims adjuster, Oscar Davis, suspicious of arson and eager with his racial epithets; Fire Chief Otzenberger, sweating out his home-brewed beer in fear of the decisions looming ahead; and I, I and Joanna.

I, Joanna, and the house, not the burned corpse, but the living house, the house alive with the wedding celebration of newly married Jules Delacroix, and the bride, DeeDee Howard, sanctified, for the moment, in virginal white.

At the top of the stairs, as if master and mistress, we stood. "This house needs me," Joanna dug her nails into my arm. "It calls, 'Joanna, Joanna, Joanna.'"

"My name is Martha," a soft voice spoke, and I returned to the Institute for Archaeological Research and to examining a forensic case. Martha held my hand, concern in her grasp.

"Who is he?" she asked gently.

A Reboue? A Syvad? Maybe. But why not a Wright? A Davis? Or a Joanna, even a Martha? Would that be so out of character?

"Who is he?" the question, low-voice but insistent, repeated itself.

"Anybody. Everybody."

But Martha knew better. "Tell me," she said.

"A man. An old man. An old man without a name."

V

SHE MUST'VE BEEN BEAUTIFUL

Martha pretended to catch up on her correspondence, then she decided to finish a book review, and then, she gave up altogether and left the lab.

"If it had been anyone else, I would have kicked them out," she told me. "You remember that," and slammed the door before I could answer.

I sat down at Martha's typewriter and once I tracked down how to get the thing started, I pecked out my report.

The remains were identified as human and those of a single individual. They consisted of: fragments of the skull, maxilla, and mandible; the torso, including the spinal column, the posterior chest, the pelvis, and portions of the internal organs, principally, the lungs; the upper extremities minus the hands and the distal portions of the radii and ulnas; and the lower extremities minus the feet and the distal portions of fibulae and tibiae. The skin and a considerable portion of the musculature with connecting tissue were also absent.

The fire had cooked him until the meat fell away from his bones.

Consideration of the remains suggest the following profile.

Sex: Male
Age: 50 plus
Race: Indeterminable
Stature: 5'4" to 5'11", with mean at 5'8"

No use putting the stature in centimeters; the sheriff will just say, "Now that you have told me that, how tall was he?"

Pathologies: Compressed first lumbar vertebra; extensive arthritic lipping on the vertebrae and on the femoral condyles; antemortem fracture of the upper humerus.
Cause of Death: Indeterminable.

The coroner decides the cause of death, but the present one was off hunting, fishing, or drunk, or all three.

A man, over fifty, around five feet eight, with a bad back, stiff joints, and a twisted arm.

I couldn't let it go like that, his life hardly a sentence.

Look at his teeth. Even before the fire, he was missing several. See how the jaw has shrunk. Look at that molar, the one good one. Ground smooth and down nearly to the gum. He was more than just over 50; he was old. Either that or he ate gritty food. One cuspid on this premolar is sheared off, there's a chip off that incisor, and not a filling in sight. Those ridges? Hypoplasia. When he was a kid, he went hungry more than once.

Look at that backbone again. The vertebrae are practically touching. In the morning, when he got up, it took a while for him to straighten out. And by night time he was hurting. Arthritis comes with age, but also from long days in the field behind the plow or in the woods with an ax and a crosscut from sunup to sundown. And his poor arm. A bad break from a blow or a fall, probably when he was young. His mamma couldn't carry him to the doctor, because the doctor was too far away, or because they were too poor, or maybe because the doctor just wouldn't take him, and she had tried to set it herself. But it healed back crooked.

So, a man somewhere in his late sixties, near my age. What little money he had from all that sweating from dawn to dark he wasn't about to spend on anything as fancy as fillings. He killed the pain with a wad of tobacco and a bottle. When he was a kid, there were times when his mamma couldn't put much on the table. All she could do was to cuddle him in her arms and shush gently at his crying.

Later, when he did eat, he sat down at a table with food that was both gritty and sweet. Cornbread from stone-ground meal with syrup on it! I can smell it now. And taste that dark ribbon cane, so thick he had to spoon it out. His woman brought the cornbread to him hot from the oven or fresh fried from the skillet. And feel the care she had for him. At night, after supper, he laid his aching body down, and she came to him, and with her love, took away his hurt.

"What was her name?" I asked him out loud. "I bet it was a pretty one. Like the flowers she wore in her hair."

I went back to the report and in its deathless prose explained how I had arrived at the facts that the body was a male, age fifty or over, approximately 5'8", with a compressed vertebra, extensive arthritic lipping, and an antemortem fracture of the right humerus. What I had found out about his deep hunger, about his hard labor, about his broken arm, about his loving woman, all that I didn't put in. It was his, and mine, and maybe hers.

I stepped over to him one last time. With scissors, tweezers, and my Ka-Bar, I cut through what remained of his lungs. Inside, they looked darker than they should. Against the backbone, shielded so it hadn't all boiled away, was a small puddle of blood.

In Martha's desk, I found a vial of perfume. Martha was the only lady archaeologist I knew who wore heels in her lab. They said that even in the field, in the sweat and dirt, she was a picture postcard. I poured out the perfume, rinsed the vial again and again until it was as clean as I could get it. With more on my hands than in the bottle, I finally got enough blood for a test.

"That's it," I made sure all of him was back in the bag, and as I zipped it up, I added, "I wished I'd known her."

VI

THE 1960s

"Body Found In Fire," was the way Thursday's *Messenger* put it. The morning was like yesterday's, even cooler and more brilliant. An enormous moon was disappearing behind the live oak in the front yard. At the same time, back of the house, as if the two had planned it, the sun was rising. Above, the darkness expanded forever, and I could taste the tang of its skin.

"You have such silly thoughts," Joanna giggled in my arms the night we tried to sleep on the beach at Grand Isle. The wind was from the marsh, and the mosquitos were delighted to find us. I kissed yesses all over her body, and we raced naked into the ocean. Last night, she was back, and it was bad. "My father demanded I choose. I chose you, and you, you who were the same age and had the same power as he, you made me into a nothing."

Miguel tore across the yard, tail high, fur fluffed. "You're glad to see the morning too, aren't you? Ready to eat?" Miguel rubbed his answer against my legs. "Let's go in and see what we can find. How about Nine Lives, the meal for finicky cats? Me? I'm going to stick with Raisin Bran."

It was too cool for the porch, but I wanted to see more of that sun, so I took cereal and paper and started for the back door. Miguel, afraid he would miss something, fussed, and I went back for him and his Nine Lives.

Sheriff Wright confirmed the presence of a body, as yet unidentified, among the charred remains of the residence of Mr. Jules Delacroix. When contacted at his Baton Rouge address, Mr. Delacroix said the house had not been occupied since the spring. Mrs. Delacroix, the former Dorothea Howard, is vacationing in Nevada and cannot be reached.

The sun cleared the interstate, and its rays began the task of warming the day. Traffic was changing from the nighttime 18-wheelers barreling north from New Orleans to the early morning commuters heading south for the city.

We should have moved when the interstate came to our backyard in 1969. But I couldn't scrape up enough for a down payment on the all-electric dream that Joanna picked out in Villa del Rey, near the Hollingsworth's. We had a fight, and Joanna went to Dallas, she said, to visit her father. I wondered at the time why I didn't see Rip Hollingsworth's red Ferrari in his doctor's slot at the Confederate Memorial. A week later, Joanna was back, tight-lipped and angry. She didn't say anything; I didn't either. A few days passed, and we started talking, but neither said any more about moving. She kept on with her volunteer work at the Confed. but cut back from her night and day, on-call-anytime schedule, and the *Messenger* gave full coverage to the marriage of Suzanne Colleen Lancaster—a Georgia peach Rip had plucked while a med-student at Emory—to Dr. Robert Hollingsworth.

Heralded by the *Messenger* as a symbol of the contemporary world, "our entrance into modernity," the interstate, numbered prophetically "I-8," mocked Mt. Hope. Its appearance in the late '60s at the Tangipahoa, north of town, was ritually commemorated by the sanctimonious mayor, by the equally pious Chamber of Commerce, and particularly by Laird "Bubba" Woodard, he of the legendary 1950 Halloween punt return and now president and full owner of the contracting firm, Woodard Fabrications. As it swung through the NJ&A Quarters and the almost-as-poor Reed's Town, and urged to do so by additional genuflections, it devoured churches, schools, and homes on its omnivorous journey south to New Orleans.

Not content to see their community eaten alive, the townspeople rushed to follow the interstate. The gas stations went first, and with them, the local operators, who always had had time for a windshield or a flat on a kid's bike. The shoppers, who for years had credit at Edelstein's Jewelry, Sillman's Drugs, and Krenshraw's Furniture, next followed the beguiling lanes to Canal Street, where, they said, they could find a greater variety at lower prices. When speaking thusly, some, no doubt, had in mind the French Quarter.

Curiously, on their way down, the townspeople met, on their way up, urbanites in search of relief from sales taxes, crime, and across-city busing. Developers converted farm land, that once produced lush strawberries and juicy tomatoes, to featureless parking lots and clamorous shopping malls, so even Edelstein's, popular since the 1920s with both blacks and whites for "low, low prices and EZ terms," had to close its doors. About the only one to come out on top was Bubba. Woodard Fabrications put in the low bid on the Mt. Hope segment of the interstate—the potholes told you how Bubba cut corners, and his concrete—and also got the contract on several malls. Finished, Bubba said good-by to the town that had worshipped him and moved his firm and payroll to Baton Rouge.

As it did Mt. Hope, the interstate, stretching its enormous sterility across our backyard at the end of the decade, mocked us, Joanna and me, and our love.

In 1960, Tulane, with ivy on gray stone, was a long way from the war-surplus T-buildings at East Texas, where I got my bachelor's, or the WPA Italianate at LSU, where I got my master's, and from the red brick and white trim of South Louisiana, where I got my first job, and my first leave. As I climbed the steps of Dinwiddle Hall to my cubbyhole behind a Mayan stela, I marveled that Tulane had admitted to its inner sanctum an exclodhopper and dogface. "As soon as they realize what they have done, they'll kick me out," I told the Maya on his stela, and, judging by the expression on his face, he agreed. So I set down to read Lévi-Strauss' *Les structures élémentaires de la parenté* with more than one glance over my shoulder and at the French dictionary by my side.

"Anthropology is to the social sciences what physics is to the natural sciences," my major professor told a chagrined, but consenting sociologist. And in 1960, to me, coming from a baptized-in-the-blood-of-the-Lamb upbringing, where people talked, if they talked at all, in spirit-filled language, anthropology was a sacred quest to comprehend the mystery of being human.

And in the 1980s, even in the 1980s, in the decade of get to the top first and that's too bad about prejudice, injustice, and misery—the decade they tried to retire both civil rights and me—it remained so. "It's the search for the human secret," I longed to tell W. Charles, Martha, and the rest, the truth about anthropology. If I did, W. Charles, caught in his computer simulation of cross-cousin marriage, and Martha, snared by her multivariate analysis of lithic scatters, might smile in a polite manner. The rest would simply be embarrassed.

In 1960, at the beginning, the Dixie cupcakes at Sophie Newcomb College, the Southern finishing school in New Orleans for those already polished to a high luster, were nearly ready to melt. One of their sweetest, with Dallas cream on top, had been arrested, and not for the usual charge of shoplifting, but, gracious dear me, for "willfully and intentionally sharing a public eating facility with Negroes." A year later, Joanna sat across from me in a seminar on literature and culture. A graduate student in comparative lit., what brought her to the class was her arrest record. She was responding to anthropology's insistence that biological race does not determine the integrity of culture. In the language of the decade, she was finding anthropology relevant.

"And it still is," I shouted at the empty stares in front of me the day they said I was retired.

Despite her civil rights record, Joanna could not let go of her Dallas. "Is this you?" I asked over beignets at the French Market and pointed to a picture of Phi Mu alums in the *Picayune* society section. "Yes," she laughed. "Don't you think I look nice?" The blue in her eyes grew large, and in their gaze I knew I could live forever.

Joanna's performance in the seminar was as flawless as her ivory-smooth skin. My own, even after long nights and early mornings, fell short.

I was bad with words—spelling, and grammar—but most of all, the way I said them. A man whose vowels came out of his nose could not possibly grasp anything as cerebral as the application of structuralism to the exegesis of literary text. I was just a nigger craving to eat at the white man's counter.

The seminar professor, like me, a WW II vet, but who had fought the war as an officer and a gentleman, took me aside and told me I was trying. Clodhopper-like, I stuck my hands in my pockets, but Texas-proud, I fingered the Ka-Bar and eyed his gut. I'm the one who wants to know, to know all there is. Split open my head and pour it in. But don't dare tell me, you fancy talking officer shit, that I try.

Miguel jumped into my lap, but I slapped him down. He looked at me through his spectacles, stuck out a paw, and gave it a good lick.

"Sorry, old fellow, I got carried away." I reached down and put him back in my lap. As forgiving as he was wise, Miguel curled up in the cradle of my arms. But I couldn't let it go. In the backyard, the interstate lay across our lives, arrogant in its nothingness. Those were my '60s, mine, Joanna's, and our life together. It was our decade.

1960—"Let the word go forth . . . that the torch has been passed to a new generation. . . ." I read of her arrest and marveled at the courage of a twenty-two-year-old daughter of a Brigadier General (U.S. Army Reserve) and Republican fund raiser.

1961—Freedom rides crisscrossed the South while across the seminar table I stared at her, lost in her grace.

1962—I found her crying and damned her father, who had refused to sanction our marriage with his presence, but she, now safe in my arms, told me that Marilyn Monroe had committed suicide.

1963—We listened in incomprehensible horror to *don Javier Montoya, secretario del municipio de Nueva Esperanza*, "Doctor, Señora. Acaban de llegar las noticias. Han matado al presidente Kennedy."

1964—Fieldwork completed and back in Mt. Hope, dissertation taking shape and a Texan in the White House, Joanna and I rejoiced in sanding floor, painting walls, and spraying azaleas. The house in Reed's Town, earlier worn and faded, now glowed with our love. In the classroom at South Louisiana, I startled my students with the proclamation, "I am an anthropologist," and a year later, I had my doctorate to prove I was truly born again.

1965—The Fighting Foresters had their first undefeated season since the miracle team of 1950, and Mt. Hope lost its first son to war since Korea—a Melangon seeking freedom in Vietnam.

1966—On Sundays, right in the middle of the afternoon, with the bedroom curtains pulled shamelessly open so that the pagan sun might bless our consummation, we became one. Love powered my hammer and saw, and the house grew. For Joanna's twenty-eighth birthday, I bought the chaise lounge to put on the back porch I built for her.

1967—In Bogalusa, a sawmill town as raw as a newly barked pine, black fought white for justice. Late one night, we got a call from a civil rights worker. Invoking the Sophie Newcomb days, the voice made its request, but Joanna hesitated. I told her what she wanted to hear, but for days, she worried, "I was wrong to let you persuade me not to go."

1968—I heard with despair Mr. Louis Green, the principal of Lincoln High, where I was recruiting students, "Doctor, the news has just arrived. They have killed Reverend King." Despair grew with more news later that summer from Los Angeles. For the first time, Joanna and I argued over politics, she for McCarthy, I for Humphrey. We, and the country, lost to Nixon in November.

1969—The interstate brought its nothing to the edge of our yard, and there was the "volunteer" work at the Confederate Memorial. The all-electric dream house was occupied by a NJ&A executive, and a foot stepped on the moon. Few recall, however, the voice

tive, and a foot stepped on the moon. Few recall, however, the voice that launched Mercury, Gemini, and Apollo, and its sound and those of civil rights marching faded from Mt. Hope, from the country, and from the decade.

From the back porch of the house in Reed's Town, next to the empty chaise lounge, I asked the interstate had the '60s really happened?

Had people really dreamed of a clean environment, a peaceful world, and a just society? Had they really sung of an answer blowing in the wind?

Had President Kennedy really said, on that beautiful, January day, "Ask not what your country can do for you—ask what you can do for your country?"

Had Martin Luther King, Jr. really said in the same city three years later, "Free at last. Free at last. Thank God Almighty, we're free at last?"

Had Neil Armstrong really said at the end of the decade and on the moon, "That's one small step for man, one giant leap for mankind?"

If they had, if they really had, then why did the students at the University of South Louisiana, in Mt. Hope, Louisiana, capital of Fredonia Parish, during the last class I taught call those words, those deeds, those people "that '60s crap?"

VII

What He Was Was Poor

Mt. Hope's principal fire fighter stressed that, since the Howard fire had occurred outside the city limits and consequently outside his jurisdiction, he could only offer an opinion as to the origin of the conflagration. When queried further, Chief Otzenberger ventured to speculate the fire had started first in the woods surrounding the property, and the house had ignited from the heat of the approaching blaze. 'A house that old,' the fire chief explained, 'has no resistance to fire. The tiniest spark could set it off. And once it gets going, the only way it's going to go is up in smoke.'

Chief Otzenberger further noted that October is the month Fredonia Parish suffers the most from fires. While it is true some are intentionally set, other fires, the chief emphasized, are the product of natural occurrences. Such an occurrence may have led to the regrettable destruction of the region's finest postbellum heirloom.

"Regrettable is not the word Wee Willie used," I observed to Miguel asleep in my lap and thumbed through the rest of Thursday's *Messenger*. I skipped still another interview with Gordon Coleman on why the University should change its name and still another supporting editorial. I looked for more about President Hollingsworth but didn't find anything.

I dropped Miguel on Joanna's chair. He flattened his back in a long stretch and then curled in a circle to close his eyes once more. "Don't work too hard," I advised, but he felt such sarcasm unworthy of comment.

The pickup had to be coached into starting, but it finally did, and what else could I ask? Sixty-five was the last year they made pickups that rode like trucks. When he climbed into the cab, a man felt a little closer to the Almighty.

I went to the courthouse first. As early as it was, Sheriff Wright was in his office, but I had to knock on his window so he could let me in.

"Jimmy Junior," his father hollered. "Bring Doc some coffee."

He picked up the report I had dropped off late yesterday, and knowing me better than I thought, he said, "Tell me what you left out."

I gave Sheriff Wright the rest, about the man's back, his arm, and the times he went without food, and what he probably ate when he had it to eat. But I didn't say anything about her. He wouldn't have wanted me to.

"Cornbread and ribbon cane? Maybe Oscar was right. Sounds like a nigger."

I started to ask what did Reboues eat, but I shrugged, "White or colored, he was poor."

"And could use the money," the sheriff was already thinking ahead.

"He was poor."

"Cause of death. Why indeterminable?"

"That's for the coroner to say."

The sheriff's sneer disposed of the coroner. "The man went up in his own fire, didn't he?" he demanded.

Not wanting to think about the dark inside those lungs, I tried something else. "Maybe he was dead before the fire. He was in bad shape."

"And crawled into the house like a dog looking for place to die," the sheriff added.

"Could be," I encouraged him. It was cool the night before last. Cold for an old man with a bad back. He was alone. Family all gone.

Missing her. Wanting to find the warmth he needed to dream her back.

"It wouldn't take much to break in," the sheriff went a little further.

"Not much," I was glad to agree.

But with that dark inside his lungs and the blood test waiting, I had to stop. "You'll send Jimmy for the body?"

"Yeah, sure." The sheriff waved his hand, and I left him turning it over and figuring it out.

At the University, my manuscript was where it was yesterday when Jimmy Junior had called. It was Thursday and so no Wee Willie. Grateful for the silence, I wrote:

Chapter 3

Putting Death In Its Place

In Mexico, the Virgin of Guadalupe, as William Madsen (1967) and Eric Wolf (1969), among others, have noted, is of such importance that her cult threatens to transcend that of the principal figure of Christianity. Some suggest that her personification of the enduring female compensates for the defeated male represented by the crucified and entombed Christ. This line of thought mistakes agony for defeat. It is Jesus, the male, not the Virgin, the female, who faces death, and no one, not even the avowed Son of God, confronts death without pain, without suffering, without agony. Agony, Miguel de Unamuno (1974) reminds us, comes from the Greek verb meaning to struggle. The struggle of Jesus, agonizing on the cross, is to put death in its place.

"Funny," Joanna spoke in a flat, hollow voice from the hospital bed. "You are the one who always talks about death; now I am the one who is dying."

I couldn't put off the blood test any longer. I went to the lab, but I didn't say anything to the dark green bag still on the table.

The technician in the Chemistry Department knew me because his mother, when she was a giggling coed, with braces still on her teeth, had been my student. When I phoned, he recited the results of his test. I thanked him and asked that he pass on my regards to his mother. He said he would and hung up.

I called the sheriff. With what the technician had told me and with the feeling I had, I couldn't put it any other way but officially, so I said, "I received an assay on a blood sample from the Howard corpse and will send you an additional memorandum. The analysis indicates an alcoholic content of approximately .25."

"In Louisiana," the sheriff snapped back, ".1 is drunk."

"And an alcoholic content of .3," I continued, "will render a person unconscious."

We were both silent, then, my voice tight, I said. "I didn't tell you earlier, Sheriff, but the inside of his lungs was black with soot."

"So?" the sheriff questioned.

"So, he died drunk, breathing fire."

"The fire he set," the sheriff finished it.

"He died drunk, breathing fire, but . . ."

"But what?,"

"He died drunk, breathing the fire, but . . ." And I collapsed. "Sheriff, come get him, will you? Send Jimmy Junior, will you? Sheriff?"

VIII

DEATH'S FACE

I was back with my manuscript. What was I doing? Writing about death? If Jesus, in Mexico, was struggling to put death in its place, how could I, in Mt. Hope, do the same?

The phone rang. I reached over to Willie's desk, where, flanked by the Beechnut on one side and on the other by the Penthouse Pet-of-the-Month, the phone rang again.

"Hold the line for Mr. Davis," a sweet voice commanded, so I did.

"Oscar Davis." His voice was anything but sweet. "That nigger at the Howards'? You say he was drunk when he torched the house?"

I didn't ask how he obtained the report so quickly, or how anyone could get so mean so young, and I didn't say anything about anyone setting something afire. Instead, I said, "The alcoholic content of the deceased's blood exceeded the one-tenth of 1 percent that is defined in Louisiana as legally intoxicating."

"OK, OK," the impatient voice paused. When it came back, the sound was almost civilized. "Sheriff Wright highly recommends you."

Well, I thought, I highly recommend Sheriff Wright.

"I have a proposition I would like to discuss with you."

What proposition would that be? Sign up for a lynching party?

"If it is convenient, I want to stop by now."

"All right."

"You're in . . . ."

"Freiburg Hall. It's on Woodard Drive," and looking at my

manuscript, and not wanting Oscar anywhere near, I added, "I'll meet you out front."

Ten minutes later, I was in Oscar's Crown Victoria headed back once more to the Howards'. The ride was slower, but Oscar talked more. Which was worse? Jimmy's driving or Oscar's talking?

"Mr., or perhaps I should say, Monsieur," Oscar smirked, "Delacroix has a homeowner's policy with us. He purchased it through Mr. Percy. Mr. Percy has a weakness for people who consider themselves prominent. If Delacroix had approached Uncle Joe or me, we would have been more circumspect," Oscar assured me. I assured myself that a Delacroix wouldn't be caught dead doing business with a Syvad.

"In any case, the client has coverage on the house and its contents, with a special amendment to include a stamp collection and a dinner and tea service. Altogether, the amount insured approximates to a half million dollars."

"A lot of money."

"A considerable sum. Naturally, when the client called this morning, we explained that normal business procedure compels us to conduct a preliminary investigation. Of course," and Davisian civilization, always precarious, degenerated in Syvadian barbarism, "Monsieur Delacroix didn't like that worth a shit."

Oscar Davis laughed. I guess that was what it was. The sound reminded me of a cross between a jackass and a hyena.

Barely in control of his glee, Oscar got to the point, or close to it, "The sheriff said you had worked on a similar case."

"It was a camp down on Bayou Benoit. It burned, and the owner filed a claim for the contents. Which included, among other things, two shotguns and a coon dog. I excavated the site and found poker chips, beer cans, and whiskey bottles. But no shotguns and no coon dog."

"This would be a bigger job," Oscar warned.

"It would be," I replied.

At the rise, the house was waiting. At the front gate, I stopped to look for Joanna, but Oscar, impatient, urged, "Come on."

Through the open door, at the top of the stairs, above the milling guests, I looked for her and called her name, "Joanna?"

"Are you listening?" Oscar complained.

"Yes," I said, but Joanna didn't answer. "According to the chief, the fire started in the woods."

"The chief wouldn't fart without first checking with the Howards. Come on."

We circled the house and went into the burned timber in the back.

"See how the limbs facing the house are burned down nearly to the trunk, while the ones opposite are twice as long. And look at the trunk. The charring on the house side is deeper by an inch or more. Here, see, on this one, the bark away from the house is hardly scorched."

Oscar had the temperament of a cottonmouth snake, but he was no fool.

"Another thing the chief said," and the contempt thick in his voice, Oscar quoted, "the fire may have been the results of 'natural occurrences.' What the hell does he mean, 'natural occurrences'? Lightning? There hasn't been a cloud in the sky all month. And no wind. That's another thing. No wind. Come on."

Back at the house, Oscar continued his lecture, "On a still night like Tuesday's, a fire will spread evenly in all directions." With an outstretched arm sweeping the horizon, he turned in a tight circle. "In the back, the creek stopped the blaze, and, on the two sides, the firebreak the dozers plowed contained it, and in the front, the fire couldn't jump the highway. The house is at near center." Oscar jabbed a finger at his feet. The fire started here, and Jules Delacroix paid that nigger to do it."

On the way back to town, Oscar gave me my instructions. "I want you to go through the house with a fine-tooth comb. I want to know what's there and what's not."

"I'll need a permit."

"Permit crap. I'll tell Delacroix we ain't payin' his French ass a cent until you're finished. When can you start?"

"Tomorrow."

"How long will it take?"

"A week."

"That long? Can't you do it quicker?"

"No."

"How much is it going to cost me?"

I wanted to say an arm and a leg, but replied, "I'll give you an estimate tonight." I added, just so he'd know. "It won't be cheap."

At the edge of the campus, Oscar, finished with me for the moment and impatient to go wherever he had to go, said "Can I drop you here?"

I slammed the door of the Crown Victoria and set off for my office. Why had Joanna not been at the house? Where was she? "Joanna?"

At the Institute for Archaeological Research, Martha was at

her desk. "They came for your friend. You didn't bring another, did you?" and she smiled.

Martha's smile was her best part. Not that the other parts were not nice, nice and developed. So developed in fact, that in the field, they caused anxiety or anticipation, depending on the viewer, as to the distinct possibility they might spring lose from their halter. But for me, on the spiritual side of sixty-five, it was her smile. Her slightly protruding lips gave the smile a head start, and the two crinkles on either side of her mouth carried the smile up to her eyes, and they sparkled with delight upon its arrival. When Martha smiled, I always wanted to smile back, which I did.

"Sorry to disappoint you. But to make up for it, I brought you this." I handed her a small package I had gift wrapped at Mt. Hope's most exclusive shoppe, "La Femme Fatale."

"Oh, what is it? I love to get presents," the little girl in her bubbled.

"Open it and see," I grinned in reply.

"You've wrapped it so lovely I hate to spoil it."

"Go ahead," I urged, not thinking it necessary to correct her about the wrapping.

"How did you know this is my scent?" she asked, as she lifted the vial out of its golden vestments.

"I guessed," again thinking it best not to explain the source of my knowledge.

She brushed her hair aside to touch a finger behind an ear.

"Here," she invited and leaned toward me.

My eyes were so enchanted with the rich brown of her hair, I couldn't smell a thing.

"You're blushing. Isn't that sweet," she teased and gave me a hug. "If Mike had blushed more, maybe we would still be together. But he knew too much to blush. He was smart. An intellectual. Just ask him."

All I could do with that was hope she wouldn't cry. "I don't cry," she read my mind. "Martha Nijinska does not cry. Especially she does not cry for a nerd like Mike Durrell."

Penn State kept Durrell and let Nijinska go. But Martha was determined to prove they were wrong. Her determination took away the smile and caused her to say, "You brought me perfume. What do you want?"

I started to protest, but with Durrell and me, men together, Martha knew better. "Go ahead. Tell me. But no more bodies. OK?"

I explained the job at the Howards' but didn't go into the details as to why.

"You need help?"

"I could use some equipment."

"Let me change, and I'll help you load."

In a minute, Martha returned in her jeans, and she looked even better. The job didn't require much equipment, but she was thorough. Together, we loaded in my truck two screens, one with a half inch and the other with a quarter inch mesh, a pointed spade, a flat blade shovel, three trowels of different widths, several brushes, a tape and a rule, clip board and paper, a pack of Ziplock bags, and a Marks-a-lot.

"Here's the camera, but you buy your own film," Martha smiled and so, I, turned speechless by the sparkle, smiled back.

It was dusk by the time I got home. The traffic on the interstate was switching over to the nighttime semis. Miguel said hello and where's my supper all in a single meow. The news was full of Shiites shouting: "Death to America."

"Oscar would make a good Shiite," I observed to Miguel, and Miguel, not bothering to look up from his bowl, agreed. With Oscar on my mind, I figured out what I was going to stick him, and after a supper of cold ham, I phoned.

"Jesus H. Christ! That much!"

A good Baptist like Oscar ought not cuss that way. But since he was a Shiite in disguise, it probably didn't matter.

"Doc, I didn't know you were part Jew."

Yep, Shiite for sure, and I said, "I'll need a list of the contents that were, or supposed to be, in the house when it burned."

"That'll piss Delacroix." With that thought to put him in better humor, Oscar concluded, "All right, Doc, go ahead. I'll see you next Thursday,"

"Friday," I corrected. "A week from tomorrow. 9:00 A.M. Your office."

Why had Joanna not been at the house? The other times, Wednesday morning, and then again, that afternoon, she spoke to me, and I had felt her hand through my arm. In the bedroom, I undressed. My clothes off, I waited. Naked, I called, "Joanna," but she didn't come. In my sleep, I learned why.

I walked up the steps of the Grace Methodist in Dallas. The casket, surrounded by flowers, rested in front of the altar. A hidden voice sang gently. Her father stood erect, tall, distinguished, his grief under tight control. The casket was open, but I could not see her face.

How clear it all was, I marveled, awake now. The casket, the song, her father. It was as if I were there, but how could that be?

It had been late that night, when I called him from the hospital.

"Yes?"

"She's gone."

"I will leave immediately. I intend to bring her home to Dallas, where Joanna belongs," he said, and I hung up.

At the house in Reed's Town, the phone rang, and people knocked. I walked out the back, climbed the chain link fence, and knelt by the interstate. I stayed by it throughout the day and into the night, and its nothing comforted me.

Her father had not come to Mt. Hope for the wedding. So I did not go to Dallas for the funeral. In our logic, his and mine, it evened out.

Asleep again, and again I was in the church where I had never been. The hidden voice was singing. The man stood strong in his grief. The casket lay in front, open. I walked closer. Now I could see her. Now I could see her face, and now, death stared back.

IX

HANK AND MIGUEL

The next morning, Miguel jumped up on the seat of the pick-up, ready to go. "Sorry, old man," I apologized and gathered him up. "Some one has to stay here to look after things." And I gave him an extra snack just to ease his burden.

On the way to the Howards' the radio was playing a zero dipped in saccharin so I said to hell with that and hit the glove compartment for my 90-minute cassette of Hank. He and I started with "Love Sick Blues" and went on from there. We were doing a Luke The Drifter number, "Men With Broken Hearts," when the truck topped the rise:

> You'll meet many just like me
> upon life's busy streets.
> With shoulders stooped and heads bowed down
> and eyes that stare in defeat.
> Some lose faith in love and life
> when sorrow shoots her darts.
> With hope all gone they walk alone,
> These men with broken hearts.

I got the truck as close to the house as I dared and did a recon. The fire had done a good job of burning. The house had collapsed inwardly to consume itself in its own heat. Most of what I would find would be pretty much where it was before the fire. Except if it had been on the second floor, then it would be straight down from where it was.

My plan was to develop a list of contents to compare with the list of the insured, to produce a map where the objects lay amid the ashes, and to bring out from the ashes what was left of the Howard history of living here for a 100 years. And to bring out what was left of his history—what history he had left—when his private story intersected with that of the house.

The sun was high enough for light, so I circled the house with the camera. I wasn't going to find much outside the foundations, but, pictures taken, I set up the half-inch screen just in case. We had found him at the southend, where one chimney still stood. Not wanting to rush things, and in fact, afraid to, I started at the north end.

By noon, working from the outside and moving toward them, I had exposed half of the foundations. I found mostly nails, and I even turned up a few of the old hammered ones. I gobbled down my lunch. That afternoon I made good progress and before sundown managed to plot the foundations on graph paper for the beginnings of my map. By the time I got home, it was dark. Miguel seemed out of sorts, but once I showered and stretched out on the bed, he came to lay next to me, and before long, we were both asleep.

The next morning, stiff and sore, I was slow rising, and as slow as I was, Miguel was slower. "You had a tough day, too? This house watching is hard work," I teased, but he didn't see the humor in it.

Since the Foresters had the week off, and the Saints were out-of-town, the *Messenger* was hurting for news. There was the usually Saturday morning wrap-up of high school contests and on the church page an advertisement by the local merchants urging all to attend the church of their choice, and that was about it. I searched for news about President Hollingsworth. I even thought of calling, but our relationship, such as it was, had been a distant, professional one.

As I got ready to leave, Miguel made no attempt to hide his hurt feelings. "Look, if I took you, you might get lost, or something." With that, he turned his back on me and went to watch the cars on the interstate. I wondered if he thought they were big birds flying by.

At the Howards', I climbed over the foundations and into what apparently was the kitchen. Between the hewn stone pillars, upon which had lain the oak joists, mounds of charred history rose black and gray in the morning freshness. The large mounds turned out to be the stove, the deep freeze, and the refrigerator. Curious, I pried open the refrigerator door, and in contrast to the blackened frame, the interior was sparkling white. A single milk carton stood by itself on the top shelf. I gave the carton a shake, and hearing the splash of milk, I poured some on my hands and couldn't resist tasting it. It was still fresh. What did that mean? Fresh milk in a house where nobody lived? How could that be? I set the milk back on its shelf and pushed the door closed. After levering the freezer open, I found it thoroughly cleaned and empty.

No matter where I stepped, no matter how carefully I placed my feet, I heard the crunch of broken glass and felt through the thick soles of my work shoes the jab of sharp metal. I tripped and fell hard against a foundation pillar. Getting back up, I stumbled again and pitched face forward into the black debris. Only thick gloves kept my hands from being sliced and only luck shielded my eyes. Even so, as I managed to get on my feet and stagger to the house's edge, a knee began to throb.

At the pickup, I examined my knee, already turning angry, and tried to think some order into my action. How to grab hold of the chaos that once was organized living?

From the truck bed, I pulled out the spare-blade shovel and began to scrape the ground outside the foundation. The smell of fresh earth steadied me. In the scraped area, I measured off a series of four meter squares. In the squares I would sort what I could carry out. The large artifacts, the stove, the deep freeze, and the refrigerator (with its carton of fresh milk), I'd leave in place.

I got a good grip on the largest trowel, and favoring the angry knee, limped toward the house once more. This time I was smart and started at the edge of the chaos and worked toward the middle. I used the trowel to probe under the ashes and dead embers; under that thick coat, I found plenty.

At first, I sorted only for metal and glass and carried these back to the squares. Later, I divided the squares into 2 X 2s and sorted the metal into containers, pots, pans, and the like; and into tools—knives, ladles, and gadgets of one sort or another. Perhaps because I was in the kitchen, I found relatively little glass and none of the crystal and china that, supposedly, was waiting for me.

I pushed myself past lunch and into the afternoon. The day that started cool turned hot. Sweat ran ash into my eyes and caused them to smart; I rubbed at them with the backs of my gloves and kept at it, probing, uncovering, and tottering to the edge loaded with Howard artifacts. The piles in the squares grew, but the kitchen had an inexhaustible supply of large pots, small pots, pots with two handles, pots with none; skillets, some large enough to fry a whole hog, other small even for one egg; ladles, strainers, choppers, presses, grinders; and devices whose grotesque shapes defied any imagined function.

My eyes burning, my knee throbbing, and my body filthy with the Howard past, I worried that I would fall again. What if I broke something? All my life, I had heard that old people's bones were brittle, and now I knew it was true.

At the truck, I looked back in dismay. Despite all that I had done, that long day's work, at least half of the kitchen remained. I crawled into the pickup muttering, "And then there's the rest of the house, the rest of the house, and him as well."

At home, Miguel was nowhere around, but I was too tired to bother with him. I showered and went straight to bed.

That night was the day all over again. I opened the refrigerator, tasted the milk, measured the squares, probed the mounds, carried out pots, ladles, choppers, grinders, and weird gizmos that threatened to turn on me, and stumbled to fall, and fell, again and again, into the burned past, and smelled its death.

At dawn, eyes wide open and fixed on the ceiling, I asked what if Oscar was right? What if the job was too big? "Not as young as you thought, hey Doc?" I could hear his condescending, Shiite bastard voice.

I got my feet on the floor and looked around for the will to get up. On her dresser, Joanna's purse, as it had for a year, looked back. In her closet, coats, dresses, and shoes joined in the looking.

I'll burn 'em. I'll take every dress, every shoe, every purse to the Howards', pile them on top of where he was, and burn them. Here, you need a past? Take these. Take these, and leave me alone. Both of you.

Out in the yard, I called and called. Where was Miguel? He had taken an occasional night off before, but he had always returned for breakfast. I called again, but even the interstate was silent. It was Sunday.

Sundays. Back in my prehistory, before anthropology, Sundays were hours spent in church hearing how the rich man, burning forever in hell, cried out to Father Abraham to send Lazarus with a little water to cool his parching tongue. And all around me, the Holy Spirit descended, and the voice of the Lord spoke with tongues of fires, but kid that I was, I stayed stubborn, and mute, and alone in my silence.

Sunday. The worst day of the week. When the Lord pulls the plug, he'll do it on a Sunday.

At the Howards' the sun was high, and I worked with head down and shoulders slumped. I kept looking at my watch wanting it to tell me it was noon. Stubborn now too, I worked until it was exactly 12, and at 12, I let go a big platter I had in my hand. I watched the platter break and gave it a kick. At the truck I got my sandwich and walked through the burned timber to the creek.

On the creek bank, I took off my brogans, rolled up my pants, and waded across to throw my brogans along with my shirt and T-shirt to the opposite bank. Back in the middle, I splashed the cool water over my face and chest. The top-water minnows, curious, ventured close, and beneath them came the more cautious shiners. I wiggled my toes further into the gravel bed, and a small bluegill, attracted by the motion, approached. I gave another wiggle, and the perch, uncertain, but tempted by what might be a tasty morsel, nibbled a hair on my leg. Still hesitant, it backed off, and then with a flash of blue and gold, it was gone, only to return, its front fins pushing it forward, for another consideration. Gently lifting my foot to leave the perch still puzzled as to what had so suddenly intruded into its world and had so quickly vanished, I stepped to the bank.

On this side of the Jordan, in contrast to the fire-blackened, Howard side, the sky was full of green and blue, the ground covered with a soft brown, and the people strange. So strange Mt. Hope residents called them crazy. Most lived in a community known as the Name of Heaven on a hill called the "Door of the Blessed." I had one in my class, John-of-the-River. When the clerk typist at the registrar's office, trying to enter him in the computer, asked if his last name was River, or John, or, with sarcasm because he was making her work, Mr. Of-the, he grinned.

He grinned at everyone, at white, black, or Freejack, everybody, anybody. I had to work hard to get him up to a *D*. When I told him I was sorry I couldn't give him anything higher, he grinned, and I wanted to cry. For a while, I thought he was a saint, St. John-Of-The-River, but whoever heard of a saint in bib overalls.

I dried myself with my T-shirt, put on the brogans and the shirt, and propped myself against a large pine to eat my lunch. I lived on ham. Once every two weeks, I bought a smoked one from Shafer's Meat and Grocery. I had it cold at noon and fried for supper, and sometimes, I even had it with cereal. For sandwiches, I cut it thick, covered it with lettuce, and glued the whole thing together with mayonnaise. I took a big bite of the one in my hand and chewed away, almost content.

I wiped my hands on the thick coat of pine needles, and stretched out. Above was green, blue, and sunlight. Beneath was a thick, brown mattress, and the sweet smell of pine covered me like a mother tucking in her child.

Dimly, in my near sleep, I heard the splash of water, as if someone were crossing the creek, but I snuggled further into the coverlet of pine.

"Here you are." A figure hovered over me. A woman's figure.

"Joanna?"

"I told you," the figure softly scolded, "my name is Martha."

I opened my eyes in disbelief. She leaned forward, her thick hair falling around her smile.

"Martha?" I mumbled confused.

"That's right."

"Martha?" I repeated like an idiot.

"Yes," she assured me. "I saw your truck, so I knew you had to be here somewhere. I phoned last night, but you didn't answer. So I came out to see if I could lend a hand."

She wore a brown and green knit blouse with a loose neck, a skirt of darker brown that reached to mid-calf, and in her hands she held knee-length boots with tiny heels.

"You're dressed for it," I struggled to get up.

She laughed and gave me a little push. "Don't. I'll come down."

She smoothed her skirt around her knees and knelt, then lay full-length beside me.

The sunlight flickered through the green needles. On a nearby branch, a jay quarreled and, bad tempered still, flew off, and it was quiet, so quiet I heard the creek gurgling in its bed of gravel, and the rise and fall of her breathing.

"You don't talk much."

I turned my head to look into her brown eyes. "No," I agreed.

She picked up a pine straw. "How are these?" She chewed on it and wrinkled her face, "Vastly overrated." She added, "Mike did."

"Mike?"

"Mike, my husband, or I should say, my ex-husband. He talked eloquently. Each word, each sentence, each paragraph, was perfect. When he spoke, people stopped their own talking for the pleasure of hearing his. I loved it. I loved his voice. And at one time, I loved him. Very much."

She paused, but she couldn't stop. "I loved him. Very much.

Now we are divorced. Divorced? It has such a final sound to it. Divorced. Final and flat, and awful."

Her eyes glistened. "I told you I don't cry. That's not true. Really, I'm a crybaby. A real crybaby."

I put my arm around her, and she move toward me. The tears turned to sobs. I pulled her close. She was shaking now, the sobs hard gasps. I held her and smoothed her hair. A hand came up to rest on my chest, and I cradled it in my own.

Above was the green, the blue, and the sunlight. Beneath was the brown, and the sweet smell of pine covered us with its mantle.

The hand moved over my face, and I gave it a little kiss and in return felt a kiss on my cheek.

"You don't talk, but you're nice."

"You're not bad yourself, for an archaeologist."

"And a female one at that, huh? Speaking of archaeology," she jumped up, "let's go see what you have."

I watched her brush off her skirt, then raise her hand in a flowing motion that only women can make and extract with a mixture of grace and competence straw from her thick hair. She's beautiful, the frightening thought came quick and unwanted.

Aloud, I said, "It will take me longer than that to get up."

She stuck out her hand. "All right, Mr. Old and Decrepit. Here we go." And up I went, like a feather.

On the way back to the site, we chatted like children, she filling me in with all the gossip of the Department, how W. Charles had completed what he said was final draft, and how Wee Willie was such a slob. "He chews tobacco," she shuddered, "And calls me honey."

At the Howards', she reviewed with amazement the artifacts I had extracted from the rubble. "I have excavated sites so empty if we found one potsherd we were ecstatic."

"Old Man Howard built the place in the late '70s or early '80s. I don't know, and perhaps no one does, where he came from. Some say he was a Yankee. Maybe," I teased, "from Pennsylvania."

"I'm not a Yankee," Martha protested. "I'm Polish."

"Anyhow, the family has been here ever since. They have had time and the wherewithal to accumulate a lot of past."

"Because they are rich doesn't mean they have more past. Everybody has a past. I do. You do. Everybody."

"Yes," I replied—and some of us have too much, and some, hardly any.

"Anyone hurt in the fire?"

Martha obviously didn't read the *Messenger* or listen to WKSL.

"No one was home. The family hasn't lived in the house for

more than a year. When Matthew Howard, the Old Man's son, died, the family scattered. Matthew's own son, Gene, who, by the way took American Indians from me, was more of a poet than a patriarch. After DeeDee and Jules Delacroix married, Gene gave them the house and crossed the Jordan to live with the crazies.

"Jules and DeeDee occupied the house for less than a year. They had interests elsewhere, Jules in Baton Rouge, and DeeDee in, well, elsewhere."

"I've heard of her."

"She's well known."

"You Southerners must be fond of funny names. DeeDee, and there's Wee Willie. He must weigh 300 pounds."

"Two hundred eighty-five when he's dry."

"And without the tobacco."

As we walked around the squares, I explained my classification. I was relieved to hear Martha agree with the procedure.

"How old is this?" She held up a tiny flatiron.

"I'm no expert, but I suspect it goes back to the turn of the century. It's for doing ruffles. Here look at this one. The smaller irons you heat on the stove. This one you put hot coals inside."

"Is everything old?"

"Oh no. There's an electric can opener. And let me show you something even more recent." And we picked our way to the refrigerator. I took out the milk. "Still fresh." I licked some from my hand and spit it out. "Or at least it was yesterday."

"You said the house was empty?"

"Except for the old man I brought to your lab."

"Then it was his milk?"

"Could be. But he didn't strike me as the milk drinking type."

"Then whose was it?"

"Someone who knew the house. Someone who came the day, the night, before it was burned."

When he drove up, the old man was already there, in the shadows, waiting. Waiting, how? With hate in his heart? Or was it to be just another job they hired him to do? Without a word, the driver got out of the car. He had the milk in one hand and the key in the other. They went into the kitchen. He made coffee, heated the milk, and the two drank. They agreed on the price, and the old man left. He rinsed the cups and in a movement dictated by habit, put the milk in the refrigerator. Who was he? Was he Jules? Why bring milk to hire an arsonist?

"A mystery," Martha interrupted my silent wonderment.

"A mystery," I nodded. "But the real one is over there," and we picked our way to where the body had been.

There was nothing to see. His past, like his life, had disappeared into the remains of the Howard rubble. But I would not be here except for him. Were he alive, I could pass him by; dead, he determined me.

Martha touched my arm, "I've got to go."

"Sure," I agreed. At the car, I opened the door for her. "Please," she pleaded, "Let me help."

"Sure," I agreed again. But she deserved more than that. I reached through the car window for her hand. "Thanks for coming."

I wanted to say more, a lot more, even something crazy like "God bless you," but as scared as they made me, most of all, I wanted to tell those brown eyes how lovely they were. I could only manage, old man that I was, "Drive carefully."

"I will," she took her hand from mine, laid it against my face, and traced a finger across my lips.

"See you later," I struggled on and in a moment of inspiration, added from the depths of my nose, "Honey."

She laughed, gave me a little slap, "OK, see you later."

The rest of the afternoon flew by.

Being more selective in what I excavated, I finished the kitchen and went into the dining room to search for the crystal, silver, and china. I found the crystal, or at least the remains, broken, at times even melted, and the silver, scorched but in much better shape. But sundown still found me looking for the china.

On the way home, it was still Sunday, but one station had on some good gospel singing, and I came in on the chorus:

"We will set these fields   on fire,
                    these fields
when we join that heavenly   choir.
                    heavenly
So rejoice my friend, let the Savior in,
and set this world on fire
                    this world on fire."

The next morning I circled through Villa Del Rey to pick up from Oscar's house the list of insured items that Delacroix claimed were in the house. With the list, I became even more selective where I dug, so that by night, I was at the opposite end of the house. "Tomorrow morning, Wednesday," I said to myself as I turned on the truck's lights to cross the Tangipahoa on the way back to Mt. Hope, "I'll be ready for him."

At home, on the porch, I called and called for Miguel. He had never been away this long. Monday, I had phoned in an ad to the *Messenger*, "Lost: White cat with dark spectacles. In vicinity of

Reed's Town. Call 344-9859 early or after dark."

With a flashlight stuck in my belt, I climbed the chain fence that separated the yard from I-8. I was worried about Miguel's fascination with the interstate. I could imagine, all too well, what the outcome would be if he tried to stalk an 18-wheeler. But the interstate was empty, and the search futile.

Wednesday, I was up even earlier than usual. "Kitty, kitty, kitty, kitty." But no Miguel. "What else can I do?" I asked, as I drove around the blocks. "Kitty, kitty, kitty, kitty." Finally, I headed the truck through the traffic collecting around the NJ&A and took Highway 51 out of town. "I wish now I had brought him with me," I kicked myself.

"Buddy," I told the old man at the Howards', "There ain't nothin' about you I ain't gonna to know 'fore dark."

From his spot, I shoveled out the debris for two meters in each direction. I got down to pure earth and scraped five centimeters beyond. And I screened each shovel through the half-inch mesh and again through the quarter. Even with that care, long before the day ended, I had all I was going to find, which wasn't much.

Underneath the body—or where the body had been before Jimmy Junior had brought me here to take it away—were bedsprings. A meter or less from the springs were a belt buckle, fragments of brogans, and pieces of a whiskey bottle.

So drunk he could hardly walk, he had staggered upstairs to the master bedroom. With a sense of what was proper still in his head, he shucked off the brogans and trousers before he collapsed on the bed. As drunk as he was, he had propped himself up against the huge headboard and waited. The fire, in search of its maker, climbed the stairs. He smiled when the first smoke crept under the door. He laughed aloud when the fire itself entered. "Here I am, goddamn it." He hurled the bottle straight at the face of the fire, and the flames rose with his screams.

The bed, he, and everything else crashed through to the ground where the heat took off his feet and his hands and exploded his skull. Had the fire lasted longer, his entire body would have turned to ash, but the aged, dried wood, the very character that made the house burn, insured that the fire, as hot as it was, died quickly.

Two other items turned up: a key and a knife. I'd bet my truck that the key would fit, once I found it, the back door lock. The knife was a Ka-Bar.

I quit early. Tomorrow I'd come back to double check what I

found against Delacroix's inventory, write a preliminary report to give to Oscar on Friday, and that was it.

When I turned into the driveway, the first thing I saw lounging on the door step in the afternoon sun was Mister Don Miguel de Unamuno himself.

"Decided to come home, did you? What happened? Get hungry?"

Miguel yawned, got up about as slow as he could, walked down each step in studied deliberation but then allowed himself to rub against my leg. That was about as close to an apology as I was going to get.

Even though it was more than an hour before supper, I laid out a bowl full of Purina spiced with Nine Lives, and as Miguel crouched over his supper with his tail lashing gently, I cut off a chunk of ham and, jaws working slowly, joined in the eating.

That night we shared the bed, him on one pillow, me on the other, and there wasn't a dream between us.

In the morning, having learned my lesson, I told him,

"You'll have to stay in the truck, and don't blame me if you get bored." Miguel jumped onto the seat, climbed up to the top, and stretched out full length under the back window.

"Every other redneck has a shotgun in the back of his pickup. Me? I got an Unamuno." I put on Hank, and with Miguel thumping time with his tail, we drove through Mt. Hope, singing "Ramblin' Man."

X

THE TEAT OF SHIVA

Friday, nine sharp, I handed my report to Oscar Davis. "Two pages!" he exploded. "Hell, man. The money I'm paying you, I ought to get a book."

Oscar's anger glowed red through the parts in his raked, blond hair and caused the acne pits in his face to go purple.

"Read it. You'll like it." I said and added. "There's a longer version coming."

When he was mad, Jules Delacroix turned black. On the phone, last night, he had been all charm. "Could I impose on you to drop by? I'm expecting an important long distance call, and I must be present."

So 8:00 P.M. found me exiting the interstate at the apartment complex south of Mt. Hope built to accommodate the young professionals from the city, who were abandoning New Orleans so they might best attend the business at hand, themselves.

"Thank you so much for coming," Jules grasped my hand at the door, ushered me in, and offered me a drink, all in one congenial flourish.

I had been a serious drinker. Joanna and I both. News time, we'd drink from a bombing in Beruit to forest fires in California. By the end of the local wrap-up, she'd be halfway down a scotch bottle, and I wouldn't be far behind with my bourbon. But the tumor came, and as it consumed our lives, it burned away our thirst.

"Coffee then? My Colombian friends have sent a special roast."

Jules displayed the package and, not considering a reply necessary, began preparations. I wondered what else special the Colombian friends had sent.

When I make a pot, it was water, coffee, and plug it in, but, Delacroix brewed coffee to the rhythm of his name. So in the kitchen alcove, it was the cotton strainer from the drawer in the counter, the drip pot from its place above the tiny sink, the bronze kettle on the stove and whistling, then water poured a tablespoon at a time into the upper portion of the pot, and the pot itself resting in a shallow pan of heated water.

Jules opened the small refrigerator beneath the counter, and I told myself it didn't mean a thing, but the milk he took out had the same brand name as the carton at the Howards'. Perhaps it was my look, or for some other reason, Jules felt called to explain, "I believe in supporting local industries, and too, the Mamelones have been close acquaintances for years."

Watchful that it not boil, Jules poured the warmed milk from the sauce pan into a small pitcher, and with a final, splendid gesture, poured both coffee and milk simultaneously into one delicate cup and then into another. "Until tonight, I can't recall that I have had the pleasure of making your acquaintance. Of course, DeeDee has spoken of you often and with great admiration."

I accepted the coffee but denied the sugar. DeeDee had not known me, neither in the Biblical nor in any other sense. I struggled to balance the thin cup and its equally precious saucer as I sunk knee deep into the sofa. On the table at the side was a large photograph of Jules, lean and handsome in white, gliding across the tennis court in a flawless return of an opponent's slam.

Now looking at a similar photograph above Oscar's desk, I saw Oscar, red, sweaty, with murder in his racket, slam a return down the opponent's throat. Not a thin dime's difference between the two.

Beneath the picture, Oscar looked up from the report, "No stamps?"

"No evidence," I corrected.

"How can you be so confident about the stamps?" Jules had questioned me the night before. Unable from the depths of the sofa to think of any reason why not, I had summarized what I had found, or not found, at the Howards'. "Stamps," Jules explained, a sneer beginning the corners of his thin lips, "are paper. They burn."

"Serious philatelists, of which, of course, you are one, maintain their collections in fire-retardant albums. No album? No stamps."

Oscar leaned back in his swivel chair. "That nigger threw gas over everything, lit a match, and poof?"

"The gas can doesn't prove a thing," Jules' face was dark.

"No," I agreed and felt the chill that came when I uncovered it, the rounded top, the gaping center hole, and the spout, like a single eye, staring at me through the broken crystal. "No, except someone bought a two gallon gasoline container into the house and set it down in the middle of the dining room. Why?"

Jules was black as the coffee he had made before he had added milk, milk from the Mamelone dairy, local milk, milk from Mt. Hope.

But the red had gone from Oscar's face, and the acne scars were barely pink. In good humor over the absence of stamps and the presence of a gas can, he slapped the desk with his palm and did his jackass crossed with hyena sound. "Only two pages," he shook the report, "but you tell a story."

I was going to tell more, to tell about the milk, but Oscar slipped from laughing to groaning, and rose, doubled over, his hand grabbing his gut.

"Ulcer." From the refrigerator in the corner, he brought out a quart of milk. "Doc Hollingsworth says to drink plenty."

Of course, it didn't mean a thing. No more than that Delacroix drank the same milk, the same milk someone drank at the Howard's only hours before the fire. All of a sudden, everyone I met was drinking Mamelone milk.

It didn't mean a thing, but Oscar had the envy. He had the envy of the Howards, who, as Wee Willie testified, generated envy; he had the envy for Delacroix, who, as dark as he was, had married money; but most of all Oscar had the envy that came from being an ex-Syvad, an ex-have-not hungry for his haves, an envy that fueled the hate fires until they glowed, glowed until they burned a man up, or a house down. But hell, everyone in Mt. Hope drank Mamelone milk. I did. It was local, Mt. Hope milk. It didn't mean a thing.

"A set of Mason Ironstone China for ten, including," and I fumbled for the list inside my head, "a tureen, creamer, pitcher, and teapot, insured for $5,000, is also missing."

Jules dismissed my statement with a finely tuned wave of his slim-fingered hand. "DeeDee has it somewhere. The set is not particularly valuable. A late nineteenth century English import. We preserve it simply due to its attachment to the family. In fact, the set is probably overly assessed. Unlike the Vincennes *faïence* you have in your hand. An aesthetically tasteful piece from the eighteenth century I secured during my last trip to Paris."

Oscar stroked his belly with a stubby-fingered paw and observed, "It is common in domestic arson cases for the homeowner to remove objects having high monetary or sentimental value before setting, or having someone set, the house afire."

"Why?" I asked the question I had wanted to ask Oscar ever since he hinted last Wednesday that Jules had burned down his own house.

"Why?" Oscar repeated. "Why so they can have their cake and eat it." And he spelled it out, patiently, "So they can collect insurance and still have the valuables. It's called 'double dipping'," Oscar concluded with a return to metaphors.

It was my time to be patient. "No, not that why. But why would Jules Delacroix, a successful lawyer, married to one of the richest families in Fredonia Parish, a man of considerable wealth in his own right, burn down his own house? Or," I hurried before Oscar could get it in, "hire someone to do it for him?"

"He may have plenty, but he spends plenty. People in Baton Rouge say when the legislature is in session, it's party every night, with Delacroix picking up the tab. He's the kind who throws it around, so those who don't know better think he is somebody."

"Lot of people are like that," I said, looking at Oscar, but he wasn't watching.

"He's always in Europe, and when he's not, he's in Colorado. Do you know he has a condo there, not to mention an apartment in Baton Rouge, plus the one here?"

"Oscar Davis is behind this, isn't he?" Jules demanded last night. "I spend a little money, and people like him, who have never had a cent and never will, can't understand why. He knows nothing," And his affected gentility curdling, Jules spat, "He's a small shit in a turd town."

Next to the large photograph of Oscar committing mayhem with a tennis racket was a smaller shot of Karyn Sue. Despite Oscar being a deacon in the First Baptist, Bubba Woodard had been dead set against his daughter marrying Oscar, but the former princess to the court of Mt. Hope's homecoming queen had gotten pregnant, amid talk about a Syvad in the woodpile, and they, maybe as Oscar had planned it, had had to make it legal.

"And, of course," Oscar sneered, "There's DeeDee. Throwing it around. They love her in Las Vegas. Used to, she could pay off her debts with her ass. Like in high school. I went out with her once. Not bad, but I've had better."

A wife who gambles and a mother who drinks. Jules has his problems.

"Hello," Jules had answered the phone with a voice as smooth milk, Mamelone milk. The voice shrieked past his ear and into the room.

"Mother," he began, then cupped his hand over the phone, turned his head away, and switched to French, not *le bon français* either, not even Cajun, but what the textbooks call Creole, and what the native speakers, both black and white, call *le français nègre*, or more bluntly, nigger French.

"*Maman, non téléfoner mwa. Comment to découvrir mo numéro. Non. Mais non. Moni? Avec plus moni, plus wiski to boire.*"

The voice begged, and I heard its plea across the room. Jules glanced at me, and I studied the coffee cup.

"*Non*," Jules cut the plea short and slammed down the phone.

In the silence, I continued my careful inspection of the cup.

Jules went to the bar, offered the bottle, and when I shook my head, poured himself a good one.

"Delacroix is not a Louisiana name?" I asked, with intentions not clear, but certainly not pure.

"No. My father was Parisian. You speak French?" He asked, suddenly anxious to know what I had understood.

I shrugged my head and waggled my hand.

"My mother, dear woman," the Mamelone milk back in his voice, "but we are not here to discuss my family, are we?"

"To prove arson," I interrupted Oscar's assessments of DeeDee's charms, "all other causes for the fire have to be eliminated."

"I know that," Oscar snapped.

"Even if he were an arsonist," Jules calmly responded to my account of the old man. "There is absolutely no evidence that I hired him, whoever he was, to incinerate my house."

"If it can be shown," Oscar reciting as if he were reading from a brief, "that no other cause could be operative save that of arson, and if it can be shown that the policy holder possessed a motive and stood to gain personally and substantially from the destruction of the insured property, then," and Oscar slowed to relish the taste of the words, "then grounds are sufficient for probable cause."

Oscar's civilization, always thin, collapsed again. "I'll git 'm," his Syvad core spoke. "Him and his fancy ways. Claim he's Parisian. Hell, he just anut'er crawfish-eatin' coonass, who marr' a lit'le money." In words flat, Freejack, and vicious, Oscar vowed, "I'll git 'm."

I took it out of its Ziplock bag, the object I found near the key the old man had used to let himself in.

"Ugly sonuvabitch," Oscar gingerly took it. "Looks like it's steppin' on somethin'." He handed it back. "What is it?"

"Shiva."

"Who in the hell is Shiva?"

"Shiva is a fire god," I explained to Oscar so that he could see, "a fire god who destroys what he creates and creates what he destroys."

But Oscar wouldn't look, "Sounds all fucked up."

"The circle around him is the fire world in which he exists. The creature he is treading down is the demon of illusion. Fire destroys illusions, but out of the ashes new ones arise."

"Weird," Oscar, the Shiite Baptist, concluded. "Just the thing a Delacroix would own."

Jules denied it. Neither DeeDee nor he, he had said when I presented it, would own anything so bizarre.

I found it near the key the old man had used to enter his own fire world. It had been in his other pocket, with the Ka-Bar. He had put it there when early that day he had started drinking. He touched it late that night when he put the gas can down so he could open the door. He knew it. Not as Shiva. Not as a god in faraway India. But he knew it, and it was him.

XI

THE FIGHTING FORESTER

Roper Hall, when it was built in 1900, had housed everything except the janitor and the boiler. Even the coach, who back then taught algebra and trig, shared an office filled with a philosopher, who taught both logic and Latin; an English professor, who instructed students in composition and Shakespeare; and a recently hired sociologist, who introduced folkways and mores to a suspicious campus.

Albert Finney had studied under William Graham Sumner at Yale, and in 1952, when I first came to Mt. Hope with a master's from LSU, he cornered the unlucky listener in the halls with long accounts, interspersed with bad-smelling laughter, of how, when he first came, everyone thought he was a socialist. In fact, he explained proudly, he was a staunch social Darwinist, who preached those at the top deserved their rank, for their talents had triumphed in life's competition for the most fit.

In 1953, without wife or family, Albert Finney died in the Autumn Leaves Rest Home, located directly across from the new Piggly Wiggly.

Today, modernized in 1960 and renovated in 1980, its high ceilings lowered, its windows aluminum-framed and hermetically sealed, and its oak floor buried under green carpet, Roper Hall barely had room on the first floor for the offices of Academic Affairs and the Dean of Student Life and on the second floor, where I now stood, for the office of the President of the University of South Louisiana, Mt. Hope, Louisiana, population 30,000, altitude 250, zip code 70408, and home of the Fighting Foresters.

The front office had file cabinets, a copy machine, and paired secretaries, each seated with her back business-college-straight at video display terminals.

I hesitated, not anxious to disrupt such perfection, until one, earrings jangling, sensed my presence, and, hands still at the keyboard, inquired with a wide, incandescent, violet-tipped smile,

"May I help you?"

I wanted to tell her I needed all the help I could get but, hearing me say I had an appointment, she simply nodded toward the door between the two, blessed me with another blaze of incandes-

cence, and returned to address her not-so-patient computer, which
was almost as efficient as she.

Inside, long before the low ceilings and green carpet, Miss
Eloise Ramsey had sat guarding the way. From her desk she determined President Hollingsworth's day—when he must sign the forms
whose magic secrets only she knew, when he should attend lunch-
eons with the Lions and the Rotary International, and when he
could announce he was free for appointments. She also decided
which faulty got reduced teaching loads, which received summer appointments, and even, some said, which were worthy of promotions.
My first semester, overwhelmed by eagerly assigned term papers
and essay finals, I was late with my grades. Five minutes after the
12 noon deadline, Miss Eloise was on the line. I was never late
again.

When Gordon Coleman and the carpets came in 1980, Miss
Eloise was among the first picked for early retirement.

The replacement sat at a small desk to the side as if to give
free access to the president, but even I knew that was only an as-if.
A gray suit with black trim clothed a slim figure, short hair framed
high cheek bones and beneath the hair tiny pearls sparkled de-
murely. With a smile that dared not crinkle the sculptured face, she
rose to open the door to Coleman's office.

Coleman was on the phone, and he gestured for me to sit at
the low-backed, spindle-legged chair directly in front of his desk.
The phone rang several times while I was there. At each ring, Coleman answered "Yes?", paused to let the party make a request, and
then spoke in a series of carefully crafted sentences that even included contingency clauses. Similarly, when the replacement entered with items to sign, he scanned them, wrote his signature on
several, and returned the others with instructions on how to correct
them.

During these occasions, which actually occupied most of his attention, I occupied mine by noting how much Gordon had grown
since he took my introductory anthropology back in the early '60s,
and how much the office had changed since President Hollingsworth
had left it in '79.

President Hollingsworth—though I was frequently impatient
and even disgusted with his running of the University, I could never
call him Forrest—had a giant monster of a desk full of drawers
through which he was constantly scrabbling for a lost memo, a mis-
placed pen, and even his glasses. Coleman's desk, while substantial,
was more of a table with a single, center drawer. The top was clear
even of the telephone, which had its own proper stand. Only a pic-

ture of Coleman's wife and single child at one corner and a larger
one of the governor at the other broke the plane of its polished surface. Behind his table, Coleman sat in a high-backed, leathercov-
ered throne that would have dwarfed a smaller figure, whereas behind his desk, President Hollingsworth had swiveled back and forth
in a wooden chair cushioned solely with a cotton pillow covered with
Mrs. Hollingsworth's needlepoint.

On the wall of the Hollingsworth office had hung every degree
and commendation the President had ever earned or received. The
principal object, however, was a nearly life-size, oil portrait of John
Roper, the shadowy first President of the University when it was
founded Louisiana Normal School in 1884. President Hollingsworth
rarely missed an occasion to invite all to behold the founding father.
When we did, the situation seemingly reversed, and it was the
founding father who beheld us.

Seated in half-light that the years had turned darker, the pro-
genitor held what looked like an open book in his left hand. His
right hand was raised, and a finger pointed outward—in accusation
if we felt guilty or in instruction if we were optimistic. A full mane
of hair and a beard obscured his face, but his eyes, alive as the day
they were painted, fixed the hapless viewer with a fierce blue. Beneath the portrait was the University seal. At the top of the seal
was a torch, at the bottom was an opened book, and between,
emblazed by the eyes above, was the command: Seek Ye The Truth.

Coleman had cleared the walls and replaced the portrait with
one of his own, of him. He also was seated, on his throne, in front
of a window through which light streamed. One hand grasped the
arm of the throne, and the other lay clinched in his lap. His head
was turned and titled upward. His gaze was fixed on a distant goal,
outside the window, outside the University, and he was rising as if
to pursue it.

"Thank you for coming." Gordon looked at me.

By now Hollingsworth would have called for coffee, pressed it
upon me, and inquired about Joanna, who, even when she was having an affair with his son, remained "your pretty little missus."
Without waiting for a response, the President would have launched
in a summary how tight the budget was, delivered a statement of
gratitude for "our hardworking, God-fearing, Christian faculty,"
and then asked, "What can I do for you?"

Gordon followed a different strategy. He made a little steeple
with his forefingers, rested his chin upon the apex, and sat as if he
expected a confession. I reviewed the weak B he had made in my
class and wondered if I had not been overly generous. Eventually,
his head still atop the steeple, the president spoke.

"When the public hears the name, University of South Louisiana, it sees a small, regional college devoted to the liberal arts, not a major institution that offers advanced degrees in forestry, chemistry, education, and soon, in biotechnology. To convey the true image, we must have a correct name, a name that distinguishes us from the likes of," here Coleman made a gesture of dismissal, "Southeastern, Northwestern, and, of course," in reference to that place in Lafayette, "USL."

Restoring his head to its apex, Coleman continued, "To effect the change from the University of South Louisiana to," and Coleman rolled the name around, obviously in love with its savor, "the University of Louisiana, we need the assistance of important personages."

Coleman paused, lifted his chin, and lowered his forefingers to point them directly at me like twin revolvers.

"Mr. Jules Delacroix is such a personage. He is influential both here in Mt. Hope and, critically, in Baton Rouge."

And he may have hired a poor son of a bitch to burn down the Howard place so he could collect the insurance, I observed silently.

"Mr. Delacroix is a friend of the University. Today he telephoned to assure us of his continuing commitment to our program."

Right after he called to say he was going to sue my ass.

"I know you would never intentionally hurt the University. You have had a long and eminent career. You are retired now." Coleman spread open his hands to invite my consent. "Enjoy it."

At President Hollingsworth's retirement banquet, we were all set to leave. Speakers had filled the evening with fond recollections of their place in the life of "this distinguished educator." The program had opened with remarks by the President's very own son, Dr. Robert C. Hollingsworth. During Rip's testimony how early in his childhood, President and Mrs. Hollingsworth had instilled in him the Christian sense of right and wrong, Joanna stared into her napkin.

After years of being indomitable, Miss Eloise brought tears to every eye, mine included, as she recounted, her voice finally breaking, the years she had worked by the President's side. Following her, President Coleman spoke briefly on the difficulties he would have filling the Hollingsworth shoes, but his tone implied he would in fact find the task quite simple.

Then the politicians took turns at the podium: the mayor, the state senator, the Congressman, and even a few Longs left over from earlier, halcyon days. Each bestowed fulsome praise in what each believed the voters considered memorable prose.

Much to the relief of the retirement committee, the present governor of Louisiana, under indictment for racketeering, declined to attend, citing the press of other engagements, but Jimmie Davis was there. The former governor reminisced how during the troubled days of his second term, when the "federal bureaucrats were shoving integration down our throats," he would ask Forrest to drop by, and together on their knees in front of the state capitol, they would pray for divine guidance. Jimmie then sang a new version of a song and titled it, "Forrest, This One's For You," and concluded with, as we all expected, friend and foe alike, "You Are My Sunshine."

So by 10:00 P.M., everyone and his bladder were anxious. When, after the last politician, President Hollingsworth rose unexpectedly to speak a few words of appreciation, the "Oh, my gods," rising under every breath, were nearly audible.

The President fancied himself in the tradition of the golden voiced orators of the South, which meant, in his case, long convoluted sentences sprinkled liberally with quotes from the St. James Bible, with a few Shakespearean lines Miss Eloise had secured from the English Department thrown in. And he started off true to form.

"The day of my last day in office, before I turned the University over to my most worthy successor," and here the words appeared tinged with the gentlest amount of sarcasm, "I gazed, as I often did during the years I have had the honor of being president of this fine institution, an institution that under God's guidance . . . " and here again, as the President once more glanced in Coleman's direction, appeared that tinge of sarcasm, "is destined to achieve even higher levels of greatness, I gazed at the portrait of our founder, and while gazing, I considered, as I so frequently had in the past, his commandment: Seek Ye The Truth. The truth, our founder seems to say, lies in the book he holds open. What is this book he admonishes us to read?"

To this rhetorical question, we expected the President to answer, as he always did, that the book was the Book, the divinely inspired words of Jesus Christ, Our Lord and Savior, but in his retirement, Hollingsworth came to know the truth.

He stepped from behind the golden-voiced oratory and, a smile of understanding on his lips, leaned toward us.

"I have heard you, my colleagues, say, at times in jest; at times, in earnest, 'That book old Roper holds is Darwin's *Origin of Species.*' 'No, that's wrong, it's Freud's *The Interpretation of Dreams.*' 'No! No! A few have screamed. It's Marx's *Das Kapital*,' and I have heard at least one of you claim on good authority that the book is Cervantes' *Don Quixote.*"

His face now radiant with discovery, the President said, "My friends, you are all wrong. If you look closely, as I have looked, you will see that the book old Roper commands us to read so that we may know the truth is a book of blank pages. The book of life is full of nothing."

In the quiet that follow, the quiet of retirement, Hollingsworth stepped back into the golden-voiced orator of the South, and with a courtly bow, full of magnolias, he bade us good night.

Behind a smile directed apparently to me, President Gordon Coleman, president of what was surely to be the University of Louisiana, rose in his chair, his eyes fixed on even more distant goals. I wondered if he would be as graceful as his successor when the time came and the pages of his life turned blank.

"Enjoy your retirement," Coleman dismissed me with a limp wrist handshake.

To him, to Hollingsworth, to old Roper and his fierce blue eyes, but most of all to Albert Finney who died without a wife in the Autumn Leaves Rest Home, I replied, "I'm still writing."

XII

NAMES THAT LIVE FOREVER

Even in the basement of Freiburg Hall, in my broom closet, I heard the roar of the kickoff. The Fightin' Foresters against the Ragin' Cajuns. The game of the season. The make or break of the year. I pushed back the typewriter and stood up, each and every bone protesting. I shook the coffee pot to find it empty. I didn't really want anymore, but I went down to the men's room to dump the grounds and start a new one.

The tailgate parties had begun before noon, and by game time, among the fried chicken, beer, and harder stuff, the fans could taste victory, that is, those who could still taste.

Back with the pot more or less clean, I added the coffee and plugged it in. Football. When we played, it was leather helmets and the single wing. Our big game was Lufkin, and against those roughnecks straight from the East Texas oil fields, we did good to keep their score under 30.

Its loose top rattling with each bubble, the coffee began to perk. The *Messenger* that morning had devoted a special Saturday issue to the day's festivities. There was a column on the homecoming queen, Kristi Lee Mosley, daughter of Dr. and Mrs. Kenneth J. Mosley, and the former queen, Kellye Ann Crawford, daughter of Dr. and Mrs. Logan B. Crawford. In Mt. Hope, homecoming queens, were, nine times out of ten, daughters of physicians.

The game itself took several columns; one reviewed past contests, including a yard by yard retelling of Bubba Woodard's 1950 Halloween game winning run; one compared the records of both teams, paying special attention to common foes; and a final one, so long that it had to be continued on the page with the funnies, recited the solemn forecasts of both Coach Hunnicutt of the Foresters and Coach O'Keefe of the Cajuns that the game would belong to the team which scored the most points.

Across the page from that profound wisdom was a small notice that during the night at the Mt. Hope Confederate Memorial, former University of South Louisiana President, Dr. Forrest Quentin Hollingsworth, had passed away.

Below the notice was a statement issued by the current president. It was not, as the naive might wish, a remembrance of his distinguished predecessor, but it was, as the wise would know, a disclaimer that a certain former professor, namely me, as a party to the suit brought by Mr. Jules Delacroix against the Percy-Davis Insurance Company, had any present connection to the University.

Gordon had acted quickly, almost as fast as Oscar, but not as quickly as Jules. From my report, Oscar had charged over to the courthouse to convince the D.A. to charge Jules with arson with the intent to defraud. Oscar had hardly started in on the D.A. and I was barely through my front door, when Jules called. On the phone, the straightforward crudity of the nigger French layered over with the sugarcoated cunning of a Tulane-trained lawyer, he said,

"My advice to you, Professor, is to disengage yourself immediately from this travesty. If you do not, I cannot be responsible for the outcome."

His voice paused, and I heard the other voice on the other phone, its dignity broken, its pleading for comfort cut short, *"Non, maman, Non."* On this phone I heard only the ticking of what I presumed to be a heart. "Should the suit be successful, and I have every reason to anticipate that it will, you may be confronted with a judgment of damages totaling a million dollars."

Another tick of the presumed heart, and the threat flipped to magnanimity. "Knowing that your long years of dedicated service have been poorly compensated, I would not take pleasure in divesting you of your retirement income." Another tick and back came the threat. "Yet I cannot let my name be dirtied by the likes of Oscar Davis."

After such a busy day, a day that began with a Davis, included a Coleman, and ended with a Delacroix, I invited Miguel to watch *Mystery* on TV with me, and after a pleasant episode of *Rumpole of the Bailey*, we drifted off to bed where, despite the ominous threat of damages hanging over us, we both slept soundly. This morning, refreshed, we enjoyed our respective breakfasts on the porch. My perusal of the *Messenger's* coverage of queens and coaches completed, I left for Freiburg Hall, and Miguel, after promising me that he would keep his distance from the 18-wheelers, left to watch the interstate.

The crowd roared again. I poured a fresh cup, and bones creaking back into their slots, sat down to my writing.

If Jesus' struggle, his agony, is to put death in its place, what would happen should he succeed? Once death is in its place and his agony dissipated, what then of Jesus' fate?

Go to any Baptist church in the American South and find the answer in the emptiness above the pulpit. At that place, in Spanish America, Christ hangs in his agony forever, but in the South, the place of so much agony, Christ has vanished.

"Where's Jesus?" you ask the preacher, and he, his bland ministerial smile thick across his face, replies, "Christ is risen. Look not for him here, but in heaven, where he sitteth on the right hand of the Father."

Christ died, he was buried, and on the third day, he arose and ascended unto heaven to become a name.

"Praise His Name. Praise His Holy Name. Praise the Name of Jesus," the preacher shouts Sunday from his pulpit beneath the nothing on the wall.

Joanna gripped my arm until her nails made the blood run. "Don't let me die in Mt. Hope," she screamed as the tumor took her brain. And a year ago, her agony ceased. She, like Jesus, became a name.

He died, too, in Mt. Hope, the old man at the Howards', hardly more than a week ago. His work, the fire, consumed him; it left nothing, not even a name. If he had a name, at least a name, people could call it, and bring him forth.

Before me, on the sheet of paper, the words I had typed had spaces between them like the space between the pickets on a fence. Behind the fence of words, a face took shape, a round outline, dots that became eyes, and, last to appear, a gaping mouth. The face winked at me and smacked its lips, now thick and red. The face tried to slip through the spaces between the words, but it was huge and growing. Frustrated, it giggled and hurried down the sentence to look for a wider space. At the end of the sentence, it paused to wink again, and pushing and testing each word, the face worked its way back toward me. It called, but I was afraid. It called and asked my name. Its thick lips turning scarlet, the face called; it wanted me.

Stronger, the face pushed against the words I had written to keep it in its place. The words bent, and then, one by one, they splintered and broke.

"What in the hell are you doing?" Wee Willie, all 285 pounds, filled the door. The face pulled back from the hole it had made in the fence of words. "The game of the year and you are sittin' here, bent over that typewriter." The face grew faint, the eyes disappeared, the red in its lips lingered, but with a last giggle, the lips too vanished. Relieved, but disappointed, yes, disappointed and irritated, I snapped, "What the shit you want?"

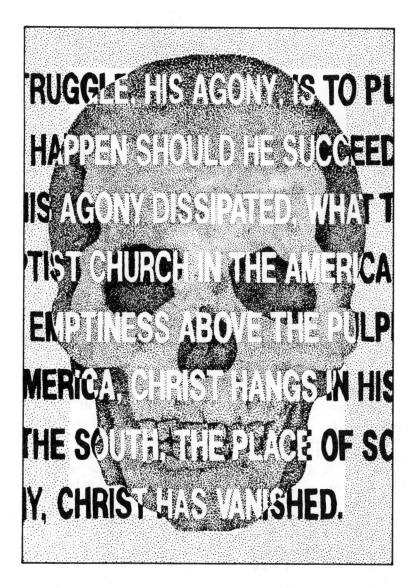

"My Beechnut," Willie took the pouch off the desk, packed in a wad, and mumbled, "Helen won't let me chew at our seats."

Willie aimed at the wastebasket and hit dead center. "Nut 'in' ta nut 'in'."

"What?" I said, still fretful.

Willie shifted the wad. "The score. At halftime. Nothing to nothing."

"Oh."

More chews and more spits into the center of the basket, and Willie announced loudly, as if he were uncertain I would hear, "Got to get back." At the door, he paused. I stared at the page I had typed. When Willie left, the face would be back, and my words were too weak to keep it in its place.

"You all right?" Willie asked.

What would I do when it returned?

Concern in his voice, Willie asked again, "You OK?"

I pushed the chair back and tried to get up. My bones, still set, rebelled, and I fell against the desk and slipped toward the floor.

Willie grabbed my arm and lifted me up. "Goddamn it," he spoke gently. "Sittin' here all day. Stiff as a slab of meat in a cold locker. Come on," he urged with a pull. "Come on to the game. Helen 'll be so pleased. She's always after me to get you over for supper. Come on," he urged, and led me out the door.

Halfway to the stadium, I stopped. "Willie, I don't have a ticket."

Willie laughed. "Ticket? Man, you don't need a ticket. You got Wee Willie Wilson to run interference."

Near the gate, we passed Jimmy Junior, standing like a stone beside his Ford. He saw me, and stone or not, broke into a broad grin, and wave. "Hi, Doc."

At the gate, Willie announced, "Doc's with me", and they waved us through.

I expected Willie to lead the way to the 50-yard line, or even upstairs to the box seats, but we headed straight for the student section. Styrofoam cups, emptied of the smuggled-in booze, littered the passageway, and in a corner, a coed, barely able to stand, held her boyfriend's coat as he upchucked the last of the pregame buffet. But everyone, drunk or more-or-less sober, bowed to the legendary Wee Willie Wilson. Some even called out "Mr. Wilson," and not a few prefaced their greeting with the honorific "Coach."

We turned on to the up ramp when Willie remembered, "Hold it. I've got to get rid of this," and pointed to the bulge in his cheek and left to deposit, wherever, a half-pack of well-masticated Beechnut.

W. Charles and Martha came by, and when I saw they were together, even if I didn't have a right to be, I was jealous. W. Charles wore his shirt unbuttoned to show a gold chain around his neck, but he made it all right by telling me proudly he had sent in the final draft of his dissertation. Martha had news too.

She slipped her arm through mine and pulled me close. I felt the curve of her hip and the swell of her breast. "Guess what?" she asked. Agog by her nearness, I could only shake my head in wonderment.

"Penn State called."

"Yes?"

"They want me back."

"Yes?"

"They even made me an offer."

"Yeah."

"A good offer."

"Oh."

"But I turned them down."

"Oh, babe," I blurted out. "I'm glad. I'm so glad."

She kissed my cheek and gave my arm another hug.

"Go ahead."

"What?" I puzzled.

"Go ahead. I love it when you say it. Go ahead."

"What?" I grinned.

She leaned to whisper in my ear, "Call me honey."

Wee Willie appeared, and when he saw W. Charles's gold chain, trouble started brewing fast. But W. Charles had done his homework. He stuck his thumbs in his belt, sauntered over to Willie, and drawled, "They call me Wild Bill." Willie, picking up on the cue, drew back in trembling fear. "But," W. Charles assured him, with the majestic calm of a gunfighter with a lightning fast draw, "I'm a peaceful man." Willie, himself, led the laughter, and the pleasure of our joy caused others passing by to join in with a smile.

Ahead I saw Oscar Davis, and behind me without a doubt there would be Jules Delacroix, so I said to Willie, "Let's find Helen."

When we got to Helen, a petite, blue-haired angel, the seats in the section were full. Willie motioned to the student on the far side of Helen, and with a nod in my direction, whispered a request. The student replied, "Sure, Coach. No problem," and refused the bill Willie pressed upon him. Helen let Willie pass to the newly vacant seat and reached up to squeeze my hand until I sat beside her.

With the crowning of Queen Kristi Lee, the halftime ceremonies came to an end, and we stood up for the second half kickoff.

The Cajuns received, returned to their 25, and, to our alarm, marched downfield. A pass on first down got 11. A plunge up the middle was stopped for no gain, but a sweep around the right got 15 and another first. A slant off-tackle netted 5, and the same play to the other side picked up 4. Third and 1. The partisan crowd called for "Deefense, Deefense," but, not deterred, the Cajun quarterback snuck for the first.

The Foresters, befuddled, gave ground. Another Cajun sweep got another 15 yards, and their tailback, led by good blocking, took it right up the gut to the 10. The Foresters regrouped, the defense stiffened, and three plays later, the official spotted the ball on the 5.

Spurning a field goal, the Cajuns lined up with two tight ends. "Watch for tricks," Willie called prophetically. The center snapped the ball, and everybody and his brother went right, everybody, that is, except the Cajun quarterback, who bootlegged to his left and crossed the goal standing up.

Stunned, the crowd fell silent. The extra point made the place a graveyard.

At the kickoff, the Cajuns booted it in the end zone. The Foresters elected not to return, and so it was first and 10 at the 20. The crowd settled in their seats; after all, Willie said, and Helen agreed, "There's lots of time." The next instance we were on our feet in ecstasy.

The Forester quarterback took the snap and lateraled to the halfback, who planted his feet and lofted a perfect spiral 30 yards downfield to the split end, who, in turn, took the pass over his shoulder and crossed the goal 20 yards ahead of the nearest Cajun.

What had been a graveyard was now bedlam. People were kissing strangers, and there was dancing in the aisles. The Forester's kicker put the ball square between the uprights, and the madhouse got madder.

The madness continued through the kickoff but turned to horror as the Cajun receiver, taking the ball on his 10, crossed the 20, the 30, the 40. Only the Forester's kicker stood between him and pay dirt. The kicker, a Sanchez Hunnicutt had imported from Dominican Republic, spoke English better than he tackled. The runner put on a nifty move designed to elude the grasp of the most talented player, but Sanchez, who had his eyes glued shut, ran straight into him.

The runner bounced up from the collision, but Sanchez, his bell ringing Dominican chimes, lay flat. They had to scrape him off the field. It was clear, Sanchez, instant hero though he was, wouldn't be back.

The fireworks over, the two teams went back to their earlier three yards and a cloud of dust, and the third quarter came and went without further scoring. Deep in the fourth, it was the same story. The Cajuns went with their sweep but were lucky to get back to scrimmage. The Foresters went with the halfback pass, but the halfback ate the ball and joined Sanchez on his stretcher.

With a minute left in the game, the Foresters found themselves with the ball on their 30. Much to the disgust of Willie, who called for a pass, they went up the middle of the line and had to struggle for two, but a draw got them a first on their 45, and a pitch out carried them to midfield. On the next play, the tailback, going wide, cut back in and with a strong, second effort, got another first at the Cajun 40.

The chains moved, the clock started, and the predictable up-the-middle got the predictable two, this time the draw yielded only five, and the pitch out even less. So it was fourth and three, the ball on the 33, and worst, only fifteen seconds left on the clock.

The Forester bench was chaos. Hunnicutt yanked off his headphones to shout at an assistant. The assistant disappeared into a mass of players.

"Pass!" Willie shouted and Helen, the petite, blue-haired angel, commanded, "Goddamn it, throw that thing!"

From out of the mass, a clean jersey ran on to the field. "Who in God's green earth?" Willie tore at his mangled program. The announcer scrambled about, "Substituting for Sanchez is . . . is . . . "

Even after the kick, no one knew the kicker's name. By then no one cared. The kick got off the ground, but that's about all it did. The ball wobbled off to the left like a wounded duck and collapsed on the 20, far short of the glory that might await the one responsible for its lack of success. Three points would have bestowed upon him a name, a name that would have lived forever. Instead, he became an embarrassment, quickly forgotten and, if remembered at all, was "You know, that guy who could have won the game for us but fucked up."

XIII

I DON'T LIKE THIS KIND OF LIVING

That was a year ago. Today is a morning like that morning a year ago when I first heard of the fire and first saw him, or what his work left of him, in the ashes of the Howards' past. Today is a morning like that morning—her closet is still full of shoes, and purses, and the blue silk Joanna wore to look her best. Today is like back then, a year ago, but different. A year makes a difference. It makes a difference, a year, a whole year passing. Maybe it is because it puts back then further back, makes it more of a then and less of a now, and that helps.

"A beautiful day," I observe to Miguel out in the yard where we picked up the *Messenger*. Hungry and not in the mood for observations about esthetics, Miguel shakes his paws in disgust at the cold, October dew. The sun has already cleared the interstate, and the lanes thicken with traffic heading south to New Orleans. To the north, smoke rises from the NJ&A.

"What's your hurry?" I ask Miguel who parades back and forth on the front door steps. "We retirees are men of leisure. We sleep late and go to bed early." Miguel rubs against my legs in what I take to be a gesture of solidarity.

In the kitchen, the local disc jockey stumbles over Gorbachev's name to bring the 7:00 A.M. news to a merciful end. "WKSL, the voice of the Florida Parishes, the station that has it all, news, sports weather, and the very best in country music."

"Where have I heard that before?" I reach under the counter for the Cat Chow.

"Here's one from out of the past."

"Your past or mine?"

"One of the all time giants of country music."

"Ronnie Milsap? Kenny Rodgers?" I ask sarcastically and shake the Chow into Miguel's bowl.

"The great Hank Williams."

"Sonuvabitch." I almost drop the bowl. "Sonuvabitch," I repeat. Sure enough, there he is, Hank, himself.

> I've never seen a night so long,
> When time goes crawling by.
> The moon just went behind a cloud
> To hide its face and cry.

I stand like an idiot, gaping at the radio, with a bowl full of Purina Cat Chow. His record played to the end, Hank keeps singing in my head.

> The moon just went behind a cloud
> To hide its face and cry.

"This hour of solid gold country music is brought to you by Percy-Davis Insurance bringing hope to the people of Mt. Hope since 1950. Here is another one of solid gold: Barbara Mandrell, "I Was Country When Country Wasn't Cool.""

"Now, where have I heard that before?" I ask Miguel, and hand him, finally, his breakfast.

I shake out my own breakfast into a bowl and reach into the refrigerator for milk—Kleinpeter's from Baton Rouge. A year ago, ever since I found that quart left at the Howards' and saw both

Jules and Oscar drink it, I stopped buying Mamelone. It doesn't mean a thing, of course, but I've been sleeping better ever since.

"You didn't take long to finish that," I say to Miguel as he leads the way to the back porch. "Don't think you're going to get any of mine. I'm hungry." I spoon cereal toward my face and unfold the *Messenger* at the same time.

The front page, of course, is homecoming:

> Buffy Amanda Waguespack, daughter of Dr. and Mrs. James J. Waguespack, shown here with the former queen, Kristi Lee Mosely, daughter of Dr. and Mrs. Kenneth J. Mosley, will assume her reign today during halftime ceremonies.
>
> This Saturday, Hunnicutt, who has managed to keep the wolves at bay for another season, promises, according to the *Messenger* "a hard fought game" and predicates "victory to the team making the least mistakes."

"The coach is a daring man." I remark to Miguel. Inside, the editorial lauds

> the valiant efforts of President Gordon Coleman to effect a change of the University's name to synchronize with its rise to national, if not international stature. Narrow, self-serving opposition from LSU continues to stymie President Coleman from achieving what the people of the state of Louisiana recognize as only fair.

On the last page, is a small notice that despite lengthy delays the trial of well-known lawyer and lobbyist, Mr. Jules Delacroix, is set for Friday.

The delays have been lengthy. Everywhere, the wheel of justice grinds slow, but in Louisiana, it leaves a lot of lumps.

Not wanting to tangle with Delacroix, who, after all, has friends in both sugar and oil, the D.A., citing the difficulties of proving arson, to say nothing of the intent to defraud, stalled time and again. But Oscar, stubborn as any of us, kept the prosecutor's feet to the fire. Even on Sunday, at the First Baptist, when the D.A., at the end of the Men's Bible Class, tried to grab a smoke before the sermon, Oscar raised the case, going over the details; the size of the insurance policy, the apparent absences of the stamp collection *and* of the china service, which Oscar continued to insist had great value, the reputed poor state of Delacroix's finances, the presence of the gasoline can, and, of course, him, Oscar's "nigger," who Oscar said, thanks to me, had a Howard key to let himself in. If the D.A.

protested there was no evidence of a connection between the body
found in the ashes and Delacroix, Oscar, himself a bleached Syvad,
smirked that through his mother Delacroix had more than just a
tie with Freejacks.

Also, while Jules had powerful friends, he had powerful
enemies, the local ones that he had inherited through DeeDee's
family, and the state ones he had made himself through his lobby-
ing in Baton Rouge. So the D.A. ran out of stalls, and Friday is the
day.

"Things are coming to an end." I set the empty cereal bowl
down for Miguel, who disdains a sniff at the edge, and then with a
look, telling me that after all he, Don Miguel de Unamuno, has no
taste for such common trifles, he leaps to the middle of the chaise
lounge and proceeds with his morning wash.

For my part, I get out the Ka-Bar and go to work on my nails.
During the summer, I finished the manuscript, that is, I polished
the last chapter, compiled the bibliography, wrote a prologue to
make certain matters clear, and decided to call the thing, *Being-in-
Christ and the Social Construction of Death in Spanish America and the
American South.* Having exhausted myself on the title, I got hung up
on the dedication.

I couldn't dedicate it to Joanna. Why Not? She's worthy of it,
her father demanded in my head. More than worthy of it, I agreed.
But I couldn't.

> Hear that lonesome whip-poor-will.
> He sounds too blue to fly.
> The midnight train is whining low.
> I'm so lonesome I could cry.

I wanted to dedicate it to him. I knew him literally inside out.
From his one good molar to the dark in his lungs, from the Shiva
in his pocket to the whiskey in his blood, I knew him. I knew everything except his name. And because I didn't know his name, I
wanted to dedicate it to him, so death could not take him, so he
would live in my dedication. Besides, we no-names and fuck-ups
have to stick together.

In the end, I mailed the manuscript off without a dedication.
I sent it to a fellow at LSU. An anthropologist like me. I met him
last January when Martha and I drove to Baton Rouge for the
Louisiana Archaeological Society meeting. Seemed pretty nice.
Edits a journal, so I asked him to take a look. Said he would, so I
sent it to him. Seemed pretty nice. Not like most of that LSU bunch.
Always talking about being among the top thirty universities in the

nation. Top thirty? Hell, they can't get the cowshit out from between their toes, much less be in the top thirty.

So I sent it to this guy. Seemed pretty nice. Maybe I ought to give him a call.

Oscar said he'd call today. He wants to go over what I might say at the trial. Wants me to get it straight. Last time we talked, I got pissed.

"Oscar, listen. He died alone, died a stranger, died naked. Even the key in his pocket belonged to someone else, the key in his pocket and the whiskey in his blood. Only Shiva, a god he never saw, was his.

"What he left was his bones. He didn't leave any history, so I've got to give him some. Unless I write about him, he's gone. Oscar, listen. Listen, damn it. I've got to call his name.

"You can't like a guy who burns down houses. Even if he is hired to do it. But it is not right that he is dead and no one knows him. That's not right, Oscar. Do you hear me? That's not right.

"I've got to make them understand that he was only a poor bastard who got caught up in other people's plans. He got snared in another man's thoughts, and he died.

"Maybe he decided to quit, to quit in a big way. You ever think of doing that, Oscar? Going up in your own fire? Starting a big blaze and walking right into it?"

Oscar didn't answer. He didn't say anything. There was this long silence. Then, in a voice that didn't sound like old Oscar, the Shiite, he asked,

"Doc, you OK?"

I said of course I was OK and hung up.

> Did you ever see a robin weep
> When leaves begin to die?
> That means he's lost the will to live.
> I'm so lonesome I could cry.

"Hello. Hello, Oscar. Yes. I'm fine. Thank you. I'm fine. Oscar, what's the news . . . . What? Oh, that's nice of Karyn Sue."

Inviting me to supper? What's wrong?

"Sometime next week? Sure. Whatever is convenient for Karyn Sue. I know where you live, Oscar."

What is Oscar trying to say? Why doesn't he tell me?

"Oscar, about the trial. I'm ready. I'm ready to testify. To testify him. He's not going to the grave naked. He's going with a past."

Oscar's not talking. Come on, Oscar. What is it?

"What? Oscar?"

Here it comes.

"What do you mean there's not going to be a trial? Why not? Why not, Oscar, why not? I'm ready. I know what to say."

No trial. No trial.

"No trial? No trial? The D.A. has changed his mind? Can he do that? There's got to be a trial. Why not? Not enough evidence? Hell, Oscar, we've been through all of that. You think the D.A.'s right? Why the sudden switch, Oscar? Why the sudden switch? Jules will drop his suit? If he is convicted, can he sue you? Not for libel. But if he is not convicted, he'll suit the hell out of you? We knew that before. Before the trial. The trial that's not going to be. You said, 'We'll nail his Parisian butt to the wall.' That's what you said. Now, why are you changing your mind? DeeDee called you, didn't she? Going to let you have some? Is that what she said, Oscar? Going to let you have a sniff of her ass? Hell, yes, I'm upset. What about him, Oscar? What about the old man Jules hired to burn down his house so he could play the big shot and pick up the tab? What about him? Don't you care?"

No trial. No past. No life.

"All right. All right. No trial. The son of a bitch will lay in his grave as naked as when he was born. But when he was born, he had hands and feet. Now he doesn't even have a head. All right. Yeah. Sometime next week. Whatever suits Karyn Sue."

I hang up the phone and go back to the porch. Miguel is curled up in Joanna's chair. I look across the yard to the interstate.

> The silence of a falling star
> Lights up a purple sky,
> And as I wonder where you are
> I'm so lonesome I could cry.

The phone rings. The interstate is empty. The phone rings and rings. There's a knock on the door and another. I step off the porch and walk through the yard to climb the chain link fence. I press against the interstate, and its nothing comforts me.

EPILOGUE

"Who? Dr. Nijinska? How are you? Yes, we met last spring. At the LAS meeting. I have at this very moment finished the manuscript. What do I think? I'll tell you what I think. It makes me want to speak out, to join my words with his, and to speak out against anonymity, to cry 'No' to death. Dr. Nijinska, it makes me want to call his name. That's what I think.

"What? What did you say? When did it happen? That recently? A shock. Yes, a shock. What can I say? A real shock.

"It is the least I can do. I have a publisher in mind. They may turn it down. If they do, we'll try another. Yes, and another.

"We hear him. You and I, Dr. Nijinska. We hear him, and he still lives."

REFERENCES

Madsen, William. 1967. "Religious syncretism." In Manning Nash (ed.), *Social Anthropology*, pp. 369–391. *Handbook of Middle American Indians*, vol. 6. Robert Wauchope, gen. ed. Austin: University of Texas Press.

Wolf, Eric. 1969. "Society and symbols in Latin Europe and in the Islamic Near East: Some comparisons." *Anthropological Quarterly* 42(3): 287–301.

Unamuno, Miguel de. 1974. *The Agony of Christianity and Essays on Faith*. Princeton: Princeton University Press.

INDEX

An index to a book that is largely fiction may seem strange, if not absolutely peculiar. I offer it as a way to underscore the recurrent concerns that constitute the anthropologist's project.